'Danticat's language is unadorned, but she uses it to forge intricate connections. The story she tells, in eight easily stand-alone chapters, stealthily gains in depth and cumulative power, and her tone stays calm, whether she is narrating beauty or horror. The dexterity of her sympathy is an even match for her unflinching vision'
Boston Globe

'Brims with enchantments and surprises . . . That final feat of writing brilliance brings *Claire of the Sea Light* to a place few novels reach: an ending that is at once satisfying and full of mystery'
Los Angeles Times

'Danticat has perfected a style of extraordinary restraint and dignity that can convey tremendous emotional impact. But in celebration of Claire, the life force of this novel, she delivers a kind of incantation that repels the rising tide of despair among these poor people'
Washington Post

'If you hope for a glimmer of Haiti, a shred of understanding; if you understand that to care about Haiti is also to lose it, to mourn it; or, to care about Haiti is to breathe and taste it and to sigh and delight; if you can bear to face the deep uneasiness of the impossible, then you will know you are blessed by Edwidge Danticat'
San Francisco Chronicle

Also by Edwidge Danticat

Fiction

The Dew Breaker
The Farming of Bones
Krik? Krak!
Breath, Eyes, Memory

Non-fiction

Create Dangerously: The Immigrant Artist at Work
Brother, I'm Dying
After the Dance: A Walk Through Carnival in Jacmel, Haiti

For Young Readers

Anacaona, Golden Flower
Behind the Mountains
Eight Days
The Last Mapou

As Editor

The Butterfly's Way: Voices from the Haitian Dyaspora in the United States
The Beacon Best of 2000: Great Writing by Women and
Men of All Colors and Cultures
Haiti Noir
Best American Essays 2011

Claire of the Sea Light

Edwidge Danticat

Quercus

First published in the US in 2013 by Knopf
Published in Great Britain in 2013 by Quercus Editions Ltd
This paperback edition published in 2014 by

Quercus Editions Ltd
55 Baker Street
7th Floor, South Block
London W1U 8EW

Grateful acknowledgment is made to Yale University for permission to reprint
an excerpt from 'Tell Me' by Jean Toomer from the Toomer Papers:
Jean Toomer Papers, James Weldon Johnson Memorial Collection,
Beinecke Rare Book and Manuscript Library. Reprinted by permission of
the Yale Collection of American Literature at Yale University.

Portions of this work were previously published, in different form, in the following
publications: The New Yorker (January 10, 2005, and November 24, 2008);
Secret Desires, edited by Carol Taylor (New York: Washington Square Press, 2005);
The Book of Other People, edited by Zadie Smith (London: Penguin Group, 2008);
The Best African American Fiction 2010, edited by Gerald Early and Nikki Giovanni
(New York: Ballantine, 2010); and Haiti Noir, edited by Edwidge Danticat
(New York: Akashic Books, 2012).

A CIP catalogue record for this book is available
from the British Library

PB ISBN 978 1 78206 851 8
EBOOK ISBN 978 1 78206 850 1

10 9 8 7 6 5 4 3 2 1

Printed and bound in Great Britain by Clays Ltd, St Ives plc

Typeset by Ellipsis Digital Limited, Glasgow

For my mother, Rose,
and my daughters, Mira and Leila

Tell me, dear beauty of the dusk,

When purple ribbons bind the hill,

Do dreams your secret wish fulfill,

Do prayers, like kernels from the husk

Come from your lips? Tell me if when

The mountains loom at night, giant shades

Of softer shadow, swift like blades

Of grass seeds come to flower. Then

Tell me if the night winds bend

Them towards me . . .

JEAN TOOMER, 'TELL ME'

Part One

Part Two

Part One

Claire of the Sea Light

THE MORNING CLAIRE LIMYÈ LANMÈ FAUSTIN turned seven, a freak wave, measuring between ten and twelve feet high, was seen in the ocean outside of Ville Rose. Claire's father, Nozias, a fisherman, was one of many who saw it in the distance as he walked toward his sloop. He first heard a low rumbling, like that of distant thunder, then saw a wall of water rise from the depths of the ocean, a giant blue-green tongue, trying, it seemed, to lick a pink sky.

Just as quickly as it had swelled, the wave cracked. Its barrel collapsed, pummeling a cutter called *Fifine,* sinking it and Caleb, the sole fisherman onboard.

Nozias ran to the edge of the water, wading in to where the tide reached his knees. Lost now was a good friend, whom Nozias had greeted for years as they walked past each other, before dawn, on their way out to sea.

A dozen or so other fishermen were already standing next to Nozias. He looked down the beach at Caleb's shack, where Caleb's wife, Fifine – Josephine – had probably returned to bed after seeing him off. Nozias knew from his experience, and could sense it in his bones, that both Caleb and the boat were gone. They might wash up in a day or two, or more likely they never would.

It was a sweltering Saturday morning in the first week of May. Nozias had slept in longer than usual, contemplating the impossible decision he'd always known that he would one day have to make: to whom, finally, to give his daughter.

'Woke up earlier and I would have been there,' he ran back home and tearfully told his little girl.

Claire was still lying on a cot in their single-room shack. The back of her thin nightdress was soaked with sweat. She wrapped her long, molasses-colored arms around Nozias's neck, just as she had when she was even littler, pressing her nose against his cheek. Some years before, Nozias had told her what had happened on her first day on earth, that giving birth to her, her mother had died. So her birthday was also a day of death, and the freak wave and the dead fisherman proved that it had never ceased to be.

The day Claire Limyè Lanmè turned six was also the day Ville Rose's undertaker, Albert Vincent, was inaugurated as the new mayor. He kept both positions, leading to all kinds of jokes about the town eventually becoming a cemetery so he could get more clients. Albert was a man of unmatched elegance, even though he had shaky hands. He wore a beige two-piece suit every day, just as he did on the day of his inauguration. His eyes, people said, had not always been the lavender color that they were now. Their clouding, sad but gorgeous, was owing to the sun and early-onset cataracts. On the day of his swearing-in, Albert, shaking hands and all, recited from memory a speech about the town's history. He did this from the top step of the town hall, a white nineteenth-century gingerbread that overlooked a flamboyant-filled piazza, where hundreds of residents stood elbow to elbow in the afternoon sun.

Ville Rose was home to about eleven thousand people, five percent of them wealthy or comfortable. The rest were poor, some dirt-poor. Many were out of work, but some were farmers or fishermen (some both) or seasonal sugarcane workers. Twenty miles south of the capital and crammed between a stretch of the most unpredictable waters of the Caribbean Sea and an eroded Haitian mountain range, the town had a flower-shaped perimeter that, from the mountains, looked like the unfurling petals of a massive tropical rose, so the major road connecting the town to the sea became the stem and was called Avenue Pied Rose or Stem Rose Avenue, with its many alleys and capillaries being called épines, or thorns.

Albert Vincent's victory rally was held at the town's center – the ovule of the rose – across from Sainte Rose de Lima Cathedral, which had been repainted a deeper lilac for the inauguration. Albert offered his inaugural address while covering his hands with a black fedora that few had ever seen on his head. On the edge of the crowd, perched on Nozias's shoulder, Claire Limyè Lanmè was wearing her pink muslin birthday dress, her plaited hair covered with tiny bow-shaped barrettes. At some point, Claire noticed that she and her father were standing next to a plump woman with a cherubic face framed with a long, straight hairpiece. The woman was wearing black pants and a black blouse and had a white hibiscus pinned behind her ear. She owned Ville Rose's only fabric shop.

'Thank you for putting your trust in me,' Albert Vincent now boomed into the crowd. The speech was at last winding down nearly a half hour after he'd begun speaking.

Nozias cupped his hands over his mouth as he whispered something in the fabric vendor's ear. It was obvious to Claire that her father had not really come to hear the mayor, but to see the fabric vendor.

Later that same evening, the fabric vendor appeared at the shack near the end of Pied Rose Avenue. Claire was expecting to be sent to a neighbor while the fabric vendor stayed alone with her father, but Nozias had insisted that Claire pat her hair down with an old bristle brush and that she straighten out the creases on the ruffled dress that she'd kept on all day despite the heat and sun.

Standing between Nozias's and Claire's cots in the middle of the shack, the fabric vendor asked Claire to twirl by the light of the kerosene lamp, which was in its usual place on the small table where Claire and Nozias sometimes ate their meals. The walls of the shack were covered with flaking, yellowed copies of *La Rosette*, the town's newspaper, which had been glued to the wood long ago with manioc paste by Claire's mother. From where she was standing, Claire could see her own stretched-out shadow moving along with the others over the fading words. While twirling for the lady, Claire heard her father say, 'I am for correcting children, but I am not for whipping.' He looked down at Claire and paused. His voice cracked, and he jabbed his thumb into the middle of his palm as he continued. 'I am for keeping her clean, as you can see. She should of course continue with her schooling, be brought as soon as possible to a doctor when she is sick.' Still jabbing at his palm, after having now switched palms, he added, 'In turn, she would help with some cleaning both at home and at the shop.' Only then did Claire realize who this 'her' was that they were talking about, and that her father was trying to give her away.

Her legs suddenly felt like lead, and she stopped twirling, and as soon as she stopped, the fabric vendor turned to her father, her fake hair blocking half of her face. Nozias's eyes dropped from the fabric vendor's fancy hairpiece to her pricey open-toed sandals and red toenails.

'Not tonight,' the fabric vendor said, as she headed for the narrow doorway.

Nozias seemed stunned, drawing a long breath and letting it out slowly before following the fabric vendor to the door. They thought they were whispering, but Claire could hear them clearly from across the room.

'I'm going away,' Nozias said. 'Pou chèche lavi, to look for a better life.'

'Ohmm.' The fabric vendor groaned a warning, like an

impossible word, a word she had no idea how to say. 'Why would you want your child to be my servant, a restavèk?'

'I know she would never be that with you,' Nozias said. 'But this is what would happen anyway, with less kind people than you if I die. I don't have any more family here in town.'

Nozias put an end to the fabric vendor's questioning by making a joke about the undertaker's mayoral victory and how many meaningless speeches he would be forced to endure if he remained in Ville Rose. This made the fabric vendor's jingly laugh sound as though it were coming out of her nose. The good news, Claire thought, was that her father did not try to give her away every day. Most of the time, he acted as though he would always keep her. During the week, Claire went to the École Ardin, where she received a charity scholarship from the schoolmaster himself, Msye Ardin. And at night, Claire would sit by the kerosene lamp at the small table in the middle of the shack and recite the new words she was learning. Nozias enjoyed the singsong and her hard work and missed it during her holidays from school. The rest of the time, he went out to sea at the crack of dawn and always came back with some cornmeal or eggs, which he'd bartered part of his early-morning catch for. He talked about going to work in construction or the fishing trade in the neighboring Domini-can Republic, but he would always make it sound as though it were something he and Claire could do together, not some-thing he'd have to abandon her to do. But as soon as her birth-day came, he would begin talking about it again – chèche lavi: going away to make a better life.

Lapèch, fishing, was no longer as profitable as it had once been, she would hear him tell anyone who would listen. It was no longer like in the old days, when he and his friends would put a net in the water for an hour or so, then pull it out full of big, mature fish. Now they had to leave nets in for half a day or longer, and they would pull fish out of the sea that were so small that in the old days they would have been thrown back. But now you had to do with what you got; even if you knew deep in your gut that it was wrong, for example, to keep baby conch shells or lobsters full of eggs, you had no choice but to do it. You could no longer afford to fish in season, to let the sea replenish itself. You had to go out nearly every day, even on Fridays, and even as the seabed was disappearing, and the sea grass that used to nourish the fish was buried under silt and trash.

But he was not talking to the fabric vendor about fishing that night. They were talking about Claire. His relatives and his dead wife's relatives, who lived in the villages in the surrounding mountains where he was born, were even poorer than he was, he was saying. If he died, sure they would take Claire, but only because they had no choice, because that's what families do, because no matter what, fòk nou voye je youn sou lòt. We must all look after one another. But he was being careful, he said. He didn't want to leave something as crucial as his daughter's future to chance.

*

After the fabric vendor left, colorful sparks rose up from the hills and filled the night sky over the homes near the lighthouse, in the Anthère (anther) section of town. Beyond the lighthouse, the hills turned into a mountain, wild and green, and mostly unexplored because the ferns there bore no fruit. The wood was too wet for charcoal and too unsteady for construction. People called this mountain Mòn Initil, or Useless Mountain, because there was little there that they wanted. It was also believed to be haunted.

The fireworks illuminated the mushroom-shaped tops of the ferns of Mòn Initil as well as the gated two-story mansions of Anthère Hill. They also illuminated the clapboard shacks by the sea and their thatched and tin roofs.

Once the fabric vendor was gone, Claire and her father rushed out to see the lights exploding in the sky. The alleys between the shacks were jam-packed with their neighbors. With cannonlike explosions, Albert Vincent, the undertaker turned mayor, was celebrating his victory. But as her neighbors clapped in celebration, Claire couldn't help but feel like she was the one who'd won. The fabric vendor had said no and she would get to stay with her father another year.

The day Claire Limyè Lanmè turned five was a Wednesday, Market Day, so her father woke her up at daybreak. They walked past a sandy pool that had formed near their shack, where a group of children whose parents could not afford schooling for them spent their mornings helping the fisher-men or splashing inside the ring of brackish water, then plunging into the sea to rinse themselves. Claire wore the same pink muslin dress that Nozias had ordered from a seamstress in town but in a slightly larger size than the year before. The cloth came from the fabric vendor's shop.

Dressed in a crisp white shirt buttoned to the Adam's apple, Nozias felt the sticky air tickle his skin as though he were trapped in one of the many humid air pockets where the sea breeze met the stifling heat of the town. Even before they turned their backs to the sea, Claire knew that, just as they'd done the year before, they'd be visiting her mother's grave that morning.

Pied Rose Avenue was already crowded with pedestrians either dodging or hailing motto taxis and tap taps. Nozias held his nose up and sniffed the air, breathing in the scent of morning coffee on streets lined with houses, whose pitched roofs were bordered with intricately carved wood that looked like his wife's favorite lace. Nozias walked at a steady clip, as if daring Claire to keep up. They passed a Vodou temple whose outside walls were covered with images of Catholic saints doubling as lwas, and Nozias pointed out, just as he had many times before, the glowing face of a pale Mater Dolorosa with a sword aimed at her heart.

'The goddess of love,' he said, 'Ezili Freda. Your mother liked her.'

Claire had never seen a picture of her mother. There were none. And if not for the class portrait hanging in the preschool wing of the École Ardin, a portrait that her father could not afford to purchase, there would be no pictures of her either.

They bypassed the center of town by getting off the main road and entering one of the épines, cutting through a narrow dirt track with wooden houses enclosed by cactus fences. Claire trailed behind her father as he followed the smell of burnt sugar in the air. A rubber-booted man returning from the cane fields with a cane-burdened mule called out to them, 'Paying a visit to the dead, Msye Nozias and Manzè Claire?'

Nozias nodded.

The cemetery was enclosed by a wall of pale sea rock. Inside, under the bright-orange weeping willows, near the cemetery gate, were the earliest tombstones, most washed out and bleached by the sun. The marble headstones dated back to the early 1800s and belonged to the most prominent families in town, including the Ardins, Boncys, Cadets, Lavauds, Marignans, Moulins, Vincents, among others. Soon, in the newer part of the cemetery, they found the house-shaped pastel-hued mausoleums and the plain cement crosses, which rose out of the terra-cotta earth. Claire forgot at first which cross was her mother's, but Nozias took her hand and walked her over to it. He bent down and, using the end of his shirt, wiped the light coat of red mud off the hollowed letters that had been carved on the cross. Claire could only this year read the letters of her mother's name. Her mother's name had also been Claire, Claire Narcis. Her father had named her Claire Limyè Lanmè, Claire of the Sea Light, after her mother died.

Nozias's most remarkable physical attribute was that, aside from eyebrows, eyelashes, and nose hairs, he was basically hairless. For reasons he'd never fully explored, he had never grown any hair on the rest of his body. A bald man, with sun- and sea-air-battered ebony skin, Nozias squatted with one knee lodged in the moist earth and spat on the end of his shirt, but couldn't wet it enough to clean all the red dirt from his wife's name.

Not far from Claire's mother's cross, on the indigo-colored Lavaud mausoleum, was a pink metal wreath with a gold name sash across the middle. Next to the wreath was a small bouquet of white roses. This was one of many times that Claire wished she knew how to read and write more than her own name. Her father didn't even know that much, so she couldn't ask him to read the name for her, to tell her who the child was who had been left such a pretty child's wreath and white flowers.

The entire front of Nozias's shirt was coated in red earth. He had cleaned his wife's headstone as best as he could. Sitting down on the cement slab beneath the cross, he seemed at home among the dead. But when he looked up, he spotted the fabric vendor, who was heading toward them, wearing a white lace dress, a polka-dot scarf wrapped around her head.

'I knew she would come today,' Nozias said, standing up. He looked down at his soiled shirt and seemed ashamed. He grabbed Claire Limyè Lanmè's hand, gently placing her in the woman's path.

'Do you remember my daughter?' Nozias asked while nervously patting Claire's shoulder.

'Please,' the woman said, 'let me remember mine.'

The day Claire Limyè Lanmè Faustin turned four, the fabric vendor's seven-year-old daughter, Rose – one of hundreds of girls who were the town's tokays, or namesakes – was riding in the back of a motto taxi with her teenage caretaker when a car rear-ended them and sent Rose flying into the air. She landed headfirst on the ground.

Rose was plump and honey-skinned like her mother, and her hair was always perfectly coiffed. Her mother did it herself in playful and colorful designs, carving simple flower or geometrical shapes into the girl's scalp. Those like Nozias who witnessed the accident swore that when Rose's body ascended from the rear of the motorcycle, she seemed to actually be flying out of her primary-school uniform, an angel in a navy-blue pleated skirt and white blouse, raising both her hands and flapping them like wings, before she hit the ground.

It was not the first time Nozias had seen an accident like this. This was, he felt, a small and unlucky town, and the narrow, mostly unpaved Pied Rose Avenue was too crowded with motorcycles, public transportation vans, and private cars. But none of the previous accidents had been as shocking. Nozias had expected little Rose to scream – just as the mothers and other spectators had as they rushed up to the spot – but the girl had not made even one sound. The motto taxi had nearly reached the mother's fabric shop when the accident happened, so it didn't take long for word to reach the fabric vendor, who, even before she was told the details, was bent over and retching as she made her way through the stalled traffic to where her child was lying, bloody and still, in the dust. Nozias had not seen such despair since the public high school in town had collapsed some years back, killing 112 of the 216 pupils enrolled there. The day of the motto taxi accident, though, the fabric vendor was the sole owner of that tragedy. The driver of the car, the motorcycle driver, and Rose's caretaker were miraculously fine, like those students and teachers who had crawled out of the rubble of the collapsed high-school building. Nozias was grateful that Claire, after having visited her mother's grave that morning, was safe with a neighbor, away from cars and motorcycles. Still, in that moment he missed his little girl more than he had at any other time since she was born. He missed her so badly that he even felt jealous of the way the fabric vendor was holding her daughter. At least she'd been able to look after her own child during the girl's entire short life, he thought. But he was a man. What did he know about raising a little girl? Maybe if she were a boy, he could try to do it. But with a girl, there were so many things that could go wrong, so many hopeless mistakes you could make. He would always need caretakers he couldn't afford, neighbors from whom he'd have to beg favors, and women he could either pay or sleep with so they would mother his child. And even those most motherly acts, like bathing and dressing and plaiting hair, did not include embraces like those the fabric vendor was lavishing on a blood-soaked corpse. It took watching another child die in her mother's arms to remind him once again how much he'd miss Claire if he gave her away for good.

The day Claire Limyè Lanmè turned three, she was returned to Nozias from the mountain village where she had been living with her mother's relatives since she was two days old. His wife's death had been so abrupt that seeing the child's tiny face had not only saddened but terrified Nozias. To most people, Claire Limyè Lanmè was a revenan, a child who had entered the world just as her mother was leaving it. And if these types of children are not closely watched, they can easily follow their mothers into the other world. The only way to save them is to immediately sever them from the place where they were born, even for a short while. Otherwise they will spend too much time chasing a shadow they can never reach. Children dying during or shortly after birth were common enough. Children and mothers both dying was also not unusual. But when the mother died and the child survived and the mother had shown no sign of sickness before, people assumed that a battle had taken place and the one with the stronger will had won. Nozias liked to think of it, though, as a kind of loving surrender. Only one of them was meant to survive, and the mother had surrendered her place.

Still, as soon as his wife's body was removed from the shack, there was the next most pressing problem – of feeding the baby. The midwife had dressed baby Claire in a yellow embroidered jumper from the extensive layette Nozias's wife had spent months sewing. Nozias had picked up the baby, wrapped her in the matching yellow blanket his wife had made. After feeding the baby some sugared water from a bottle his wife had also bought for the layette, the midwife had left the baby with him and rushed into town, looking for formula or a wet nurse. Even from those very first hours, Claire was an easy and quiet child. It was as though she already knew that she could not afford to be picky or make demands.

During that first evening with baby Claire, Nozias had visions for which he detested himself, fantasies about letting her starve to death. He'd even imagined dropping her in the sea. But these were things he was thinking of doing to her because he couldn't do them to himself. He could not poison himself, as he so desperately wanted, couldn't leave her completely parentless and have her end up in a brothel or on the streets. Already he was worried that mosquitoes and sand flies might bite her, that she might get malaria or dengue fever. He feared for himself too. He feared being lost at sea or getting hit by a car, or being struck with a terrible disease that would separate them forever.

An hour passed since his wife's body had been removed, then another hour passed, and when the midwife did not return, he wrapped the yellow blanket more tightly around baby Claire and took her into town.

Evening had fallen quickly, and as he walked through the town, he felt as though he were seeing it anew. It was cloudy and the sky was grumbling, though there seemed to be no sign of rain. The sea had risen a few feet and was becoming agitated, pushing larger waves toward the shore. A few of the townspeople were cautiously lurching about, most with their backs to the wind, as they made their way home from work or the fields. Others were grabbing rocking chairs and planters from their filigree porches, moving anything that could be lifted and carried inside. The wind slowed his steps as he picked flying twigs off the baby's blanket. He felt the baby squirm against his chest, and to avoid thinking about how hungry she must be, he thought instead of his wife, who, even on days when she didn't have to go to work washing and dressing the dead at Albert Vincent's funeral parlor, or have to go buy food, would walk through town sometimes, not to do anything in particular, but to look at people and faces and browse through the open markets and fancy shops and pick up things that both she and the vendors knew she would only put down again.

He and his wife had met when she'd come to buy fish for one of the food vendors in the covered market in town. She made her rounds three days a week, inspecting everyone's catch before filling a small basket with snapper and cod. Soon he began saving his best and biggest fish for her. On days when he was expecting her and couldn't go out to sea, or days when he had a bad catch, he was doubly sad.

He called her 'wife,' my wife, madanm mwen, when it should be really 'woman,' except he didn't like the words 'fanm mwen.' 'My woman' sounded illicit to him, like a mistress. They were never officially married. Still, it wasn't hard to convince her to come live with him. She was sleeping in one of the sheds in the market while every day she'd go to the funeral home to ask if she could help there – work, just as she had been doing in the mountains before she moved to town, washing and dressing the dead. Whenever he told the story of their meeting to his fishermen friends, he often added that he was the only man she liked who wasn't dead. So one day he asked her to come live with him and she said yes.

The day before she moved in, he cleaned up a bit, touching up the shack's walls, replacing some rotting wood panels and plugging a few small holes in the tin roof. He even bought a brand-new foam mattress and cot. He changed the name of his boat from that of an old love's to hers. From then on, all his fishing boats were named Claire.

Things were going all right, until they began trying to have a baby.

Nozias felt baby Claire stir again as he hurried past the white corner building that housed the town hospital, L'hôpital Sainte Thérèse. For months after she came to live with him, Claire Narcis, the daughter of mountain undertakers and professional mourners, drank rum-soaked herbs and leaves that were supposed to make her pregnant. Instead they made her drunk, which increased the frequency of sex, but led to no immediate results. For a year, he kept wishing he had known before she'd moved in with him how much having a baby meant to her. He would have at least told her about his near-operation.

Fearful of being bound to a handful of children he couldn't feed, he had always carried around his desire not to have them like an awful secret, something that made him feel like less of a man. That is until one day, he was walking by L'hôpital Sainte Thérèse, as he just had, and rather than the usual early-morning crowd of sick and dying people, he saw a long line of young healthy men waiting. Curious, he approached them and was told there was a simple way to prevent him from having children, something that would require him to still take precautions so he wouldn't get sick from sex, but would keep him from being a father.

After a lengthy presentation in the hospital's courtyard, and a short movie filled with the testimonials of grateful men, a white doctor who also appeared to be in his twenties told the men to go home and think about it. Of all of them, Nozias was the only one who'd said he wanted the operation that same day.

The doctor had wanted to do blood tests, but Nozias, through a translating Haitian nurse, had refused. He simply wanted the operation, he said, and nothing else. The doctor relented.

He was told that he would be awake the whole time. A sheet was placed mid-waist so he couldn't see what the doctor was doing to him. But when he felt the pinch of a needle on one of his testicles, he let out a loud screech and yelled that he had changed his mind. Nozias leaped from the table, put on his pants, and ran out of the hospital, feeling certain then that he would like to be a father one day.

He wished he could be as certain now as he hurried past the town cathedral with the infant Claire pressed against his chest. The bells began ringing the seven o'clock hour as if in alarm, while people rushed inside the church for the evening Mass and to seek shelter from the wind. Through a crack in the massive wooden doors, he glimpsed the crucified Christ, the stained glass and candle flames. Given the way that she was born and given what some people thought about children like her, he wondered if he should stop and have Claire blessed. But remembering how long she'd gone without being fed, he decided against stopping. Just at that moment, as he was rushing by, a white-haired priest held the church door open for him. It was Pè Marignan, Sainte Rose de Lima's head cleric. The priest raised his hand and hastily blessed them from a distance. Nozias gave the priest a nod of gratitude and continued past the church toward Chez Lavaud, the town fabric shop. There, he saw the fabric vendor standing by her burly, armed, and uniformed night watchman as he chained and padlocked the shop's metal gates. Next to her, her three-year-old daughter was tugging at her skirt. Claire began to cry, and the fabric vendor turned to see where the cry was coming from.

'Madame,' Nozias said, walking toward her.

He could already see on the fabric vendor's face that she knew what had happened. How could she not have? Nowhere does news spread faster than Ville Rose. Most of the women in town had probably heard how his wife's heart had suddenly stopped toward the end of her labor, yet, fearful of the mother's spirit returning to claim the child, no one but the midwife, who was used to such things, had yet rushed to his and the child's aid.

For his part, Nozias had heard that the fabric vendor was still nursing her pudgy three-year-old girl. The fact that she had not yet weaned such a big child, whose name he knew was Rose, was so unusual for a woman of her stature that everyone knew about it. Proving herself kinder and braver than he thought, the fabric vendor asked her night watchman to reopen the front gate, and motioned for the watchman to wait for her outside and for Nozias to follow her inside. She pushed open another door, then flipped a light switch, turning on some lightbulbs dangling over the fabric-filled shelves and towering spools of cloth. Nozias, the fabric vendor, and her sleepy-looking daughter all sat down on a long wooden bench in the waiting area. The fabric vendor unbuttoned a silk blouse, making no effort to shield her large breasts, which were a few shades lighter than her face.

Claire latched on quickly and, first right, then left, emptied both the fabric vendor's breasts while Rose looked on awestruck and brokenhearted, as though she had not been aware until that moment that this was something her mother could do for anyone but her.

Nozias thought he might bring Claire to the fabric vendor every day, but after smiling and cooing at the baby, the woman tightened her face and handed his daughter back to him, giving him the scowl one might imagine she reserved for her credit-seeking customers. Pointing to the sleepy three-year-old sitting next to her, the fabric vendor said, 'She needs my milk.'

He did not say it, but he was thinking that his child and hers were now milk sisters. The fabric vendor had offered baby Claire her breasts. Couldn't he ask her to be his child's godmother? She certainly had the means. She also had a long history in the town. One grandfather had been an engineer. He had built the Anthère Hill lighthouse and had helped rebuild parts of the town several times after hurricanes. Another grandfather had been a pharmacist and lay medicine man. One grandmother ran her own sugarcane business. Another had been a schoolteacher at the lycée. Her father had been the town magistrate and her mother, a potter, made clay vases for sale, which she was now selling in her own shop in Port-au-Prince.

The only thing Nozias didn't like about the fabric vendor was her reputed loose ways, her rumored desperation for male companionship. Nozias knew that his wife had come to the fabric shop often to barter her hand-embroidered baby blankets. He now wondered if the two women had ever spoken at length. Did they ever talk as more than just client and customer? As potential young mothers?

While he stood there, near the shop's front door, rocking the warm, contented baby in his arms, he thought that if he waited long enough the fabric vendor might change her mind. Would she find his daughter so pretty or pitiful that she would let her come again to nurse? Instead, she reached into her skirt pocket and fished out a few bills and pushed them toward him.

'Do you have any other family?' she asked, stroking her own daughter's perfect hair. 'A sister?' Before he could answer, she added, 'If you don't have a sister, you should send her to your woman's people.

'Do you have a place to bury your woman's body?' she continued. 'You can, if you like, make use of part of the plot we have in the cemetery.'

The wind had subsided. He thanked her and hurried home with the child asleep in his arms. The midwife was waiting for him on his doorstep.

'You took this child out after dusk?' she chided.

The midwife had bottles and powder and treated water and was frantic to feed them to the sleeping baby. Those bottles and powder, that water, along with the funeral expenses, would wipe out most of the money he and his wife had been saving for another place away from the sea.

The next day, the fabric vendor had one of her employees bring a package for baby Claire. It was the size of a small pillow and was wrapped in the brown paper and bound with the beige sisal rope the fabric vendor used to tie bundles of cloth from her shop. Inside was an embroidered green blanket bordered with white lace and some hand-embroidered baby jumpers. They were the type of baby layette items that his wife liked to sew and had made plenty of for her own child.

When Nozias's wife's sister arrived for the funeral, he gave her the two-day-old baby, along with the layette his wife had made and the fabric vendor's package and the little money he had left.

He was relieved not to have to worry about baby Claire for a while, yet he didn't leave Ville Rose. He kept his boat and shack. He worked harder and spent more time at sea so that he'd have enough money to send for her care. Yet he didn't visit, nor did he ask for her to be brought to him.

Sometimes, in the months that followed, during his long hours at sea, he would wonder who and what she looked like. Would she be cross-eyed or bow-legged, fat or skinny? Was she serene or dezòd, an insolent child? Would she even know that she'd had a mother who was dead?

As her third birthday approached, he felt he was ready

to see her again. So he sent word to his sister-in-law to bring her back to him on her birthday. And when he saw her, she was loose-jointed and gangly, heartbreakingly, a smaller version of her mother. He had a dress sewn for the occasion, one that he would have replicated by the same seamstress in a larger size, but the same style, year after year. His wife had made one just like it, imagining that their daughter would wear it for her first birthday. He'd kept that very first dress when he had sent her away. Often he'd lay it across his chest at night, as he might have done with the child if she were with him.

Midday on Claire Limyè Lanmè Faustin's seventh birthday, Nozias rushed her to the cemetery for their annual visit to her mother's grave. The sky had cleared and turned aquamarine, and if not for Caleb's disappearance, that morning's rogue wave might have already become a distant memory.

Claire was wearing her largest version yet of the pink birthday dress, and as Nozias watched her pull at it, tugging the fabric away from her skin, he told himself that this would be the last year he would get this dress made. Next year, for her eighth birthday, if she were still with him, he would let her choose what to wear. He might even take her to a vendor in town and have her pick out a ready-made dress for herself.

Guiding the girl past the large planter of red azaleas in front of the Lavaud mausoleum, past the bouquet of white roses that seemed a little bigger each year, he stood with her before the cement cross that was her mother's grave. The girl shielded her face with her hands, squinting to keep the sun out of her eyes. Even though he visited the gravesite regularly, Nozias always felt the same rush of pain, almost like being punched in the heart, each time he was there. He asked himself if his daughter felt the same way.

His daughter let go of his hand and lingered a few steps behind. She too seemed lost in her thoughts. Nozias feared that she was no longer interested in these visits to her mother's grave. The girl paced back and forth, while still tugging at the hem of her dress. She raised her face toward his, removing her fingers from her eyes and allowing the sun to strike them.

It is time to leave, her eyes seemed to be saying. Now that it was clear to him that she wanted to go, he too became eager to return to the sea. A relay search party was being launched for Caleb, and he wanted to be part of the second group.

That afternoon, he and a few other fishermen put a fleet of canoes and dinghies and sloops on the water, with his boat and its colorful sail made from old advertising banners in the lead. He liked a festive sail and, over the years, once he had modified his rowboat, had collected from Msye Pierre, the editor of the town newspaper and also a party promoter, old banners for music groups. His sail was now a patchwork of band names and long-past dates for shows at the seaside speakeasies or the plaza in the middle of town. The other fishermen had tame, grasshopper-shaped, unicolored sails, but Nozias's sails were like rare butterflies. If Caleb had been around, his would have been the lead boat, as he was the oldest of all the fishermen and his cutter, *Fifine,* had always been the biggest and strongest on the water.

The sea was windless that afternoon. From his boat out on the water Nozias saw Claire Limyè Lanmè standing next to a group of boys hanging a throw net to dry in front of one of the shacks. The boys were too involved in their work to notice her and she was too busy watching the water, trying not to lose sight of him, to pay attention to them. In the end, he spent more time looking at her than he did looking for Caleb, whom he already knew the sea would not surrender.

Claire walked back to their shack after a while, her gait sluggish in the afternoon sun. Now he could no longer see her. Even this far out at sea, he realized that he should never have told her that had he woken up earlier that morning, he too might be dead.

When he and the other fishermen returned from the water at dusk, dejected that their search had not yielded Caleb, although there was a full and dazzling moon on the horizon, some of the fishermen made a bonfire. Every once in a while one of the fishermen would throw a handful of rock salt in the fire to make sparks, hoping to draw Caleb's spirit out of the sea. As Josephine, Caleb's wife, silently wept, Nozias and the other fishermen sat on the warm sand next to her, drank kleren, and played cards, just as they would at an official wake.

In the distance, Nozias saw his daughter holding hands in a circle with five other girls, spinning one another in a dizzying game called the wonn. One of his neighbors had probably brought her a plate of food, or had invited her in to eat, just as someone always did whenever he was at sea. As he watched her, sensing his daughter avoiding him, dozens of townspeople came by, bringing, as was the custom, small sums of money to Caleb's wife.

Pè Marignan, who was often called on to bless nets and baptize new boats, came to offer a blessing. One of the town's many Protestant ministers, Pastè Etienne, also came. He was accompanied by a group of elderly women who were dressed in white from head to toe. Caleb's wife, Josephine, was a member of Pastè Etienne's charismatic evangelical congregation. Before joining their hands together to lay on Josephine's head, Pastè Etienne and the women helped Josephine drop to her knees. When they were done and had helped her back up, the mayor/undertaker, Albert Vincent, came by. During the few minutes Albert Vincent was chatting with Josephine, one of the fishermen around the bonfire said loudly enough for everyone to hear that the mayor part of him was investigating a disaster, but the undertaker side was trolling for corpses. In fact, Albert

Vincent was looking around him, as if searching not just for a corpse, but a ghost.

Nozias got up and shook Albert Vincent's unsteady hand. Even after all these years, he was grateful that Albert Vincent had given his wife a job at his funeral home when she was still new in town, a job that had meant everything to her. Albert Vincent was also the one who'd sought out a scholarship for his daughter at his friend Max Ardin's school, in honor of Claire's mother's memory.

'How is Ti Claire?' Albert Vincent asked. He often referred to Nozias's daughter as Ti Claire, Little Claire.

Nozias nodded, indicating that his daughter was fine. Despite his gratitude, he always found it hard to be in Albert Vincent's presence and not feel a groundswell of grief, especially on a day like this. Even in the sea air, Albert Vincent smelled like his wife had smelled when she'd been working for him. His smell, like hers, was the smell of death, covered by fragrances intended to mask it.

Nozias also felt ill at ease with unsolicited kindness. He was ashamed that his need for charity was so obvious, especially to someone he could never repay, except with a fish here and there or with his humblest, meekest, most self-effacing expression of gratitude every time their paths crossed.

'I don't know how to thank you again, Msye Albert, for all you've done for the girl,' he said, shortly after his hello.

'Then stop thanking me,' Albert Vincent said, patting him on the shoulder. 'The girl's mother was a part of our Pax Vincent family.'

On that particular night, Nozias felt that Albert Vincent was stretching the meaning of family so far that Albert Vincent, perhaps without meaning to, was debasing his. She was *my* family, he wanted to say. Not yours. Or the funeral home's. Instead, he said, 'Wi, Msye Albert. Mèsi anpil. Thank you very much.'

Walking away from Albert Vincent, Nozias realized that he'd lost sight of Claire. The kleren that had been passed around the bonfire had fogged his head a bit. Then there was the throat-tightening experience of speaking with Albert Vincent, after which he was unable to even string together the words to properly ask the people he stumbled into whether they'd seen his daughter.

He wasn't even sure now how much time had lapsed since he'd last seen her. But while approaching his shack, he spotted her. She was sitting next to a woman. It was a woman he knew, except he had never seen her like this. Her hair was wrapped in a black net, above some giant pink sponge rollers, and she was wearing a long silver-looking evening gown. It was the fabric vendor, and she was in deep conversation with his daughter.

He was afraid to walk up to them and would have been happy to stand where he was and just keep watching them, except the fabric vendor noticed him and he thought he saw her wave.

She and Claire were each sitting on a boulder. He crouched down and sat between them on the sand.

Why was life still able to surprise him like this? he asked himself. Maybe it was this day. This most impossible of days, this day of both life and death.

But wasn't this what he had been waiting for, hoping for, some interest in his daughter from a woman of means, a woman who had been the first and only person to have nursed her? Suddenly the full moon seemed to have drifted directly above their three heads. He felt as though everyone were watching them, waiting to see what the fabric vendor would do, what the fabric vendor would say.

'Wi,' the fabric vendor blurted out, as though she and he were at the end of a very long conversation. 'Yes. I will take her. Tonight.'

Claire kept her eyes on the sand, but Nozias could see a tear slide down the side of her face. He wanted to reach for her, bury his nose in her cheek just the same way she liked to needle hers into his when he was sad.

'Why now? Why tonight?' he managed to say.

'It's now or never.' The fabric vendor reached down to wipe Claire's face, but the girl pulled away. 'I need another way to remember this day.' The fabric vendor brought her hands together in a fold in her long thin satin gown, between her knees. 'Now or never,' she said again. She then moved her hands to the girl's back and attempted to stroke it.

Claire's body was shaking as she watched a second pile

of driftwood being placed in her father's friends' spluttering bonfire.

'Claire Limyè Lanmè,' Nozias called out to her. Claire did not turn her face. He wished he could tell her a few things before she was no longer his, but most important this.

One evening after he'd learned that his wife was pregnant, they went out to sea together for some night fishing. That night, the wind seemed to be circling them, and he found himself going around and around the same small area before his sloop stalled as if it had reached a wall. He was afraid that they might be stuck on a reef, but he managed to push back. He had not yet switched on the lantern he had borrowed from his friend Caleb, when suddenly his wife removed her sundress and was sitting there in only her panties, arching her body so that it could be aimed at him like an arrow.

He took note of her slightly larger belly and breasts and realized that she was trying to get him used to it. But before he could say anything, she slipped both her legs over the stern, nearly toppling the boat as she slid into the sea. Her body parted the moonlit surface of the sea, pulling her forward as she sunk her head in, then raised it up and out again. She was now gliding away from him, her long plaited hair floating on the surface as if separate from her face. He rowed faster, trying to catch up.

'Claire, reken, reef sharks,' he shouted. 'There could be reef sharks!'

She pulled her head out of the water and let out a deep, breathless laugh.

'There will be if you keep calling them,' she said. 'Come and look here.'

As he rowed toward her, his face relaxed, and he saw what she had swum out to observe. Surrounding her was a dazzling glow. It was as though her patch of the sea were being lit from below. From her perfectly round breasts down, she was in the middle of a school of tiny silver fish, which were ignoring her and feeding on gleaming specks of algae floating on the water's surface.

He stopped rowing and rested his arms as he pondered her new body and what – who – might emerge from it, just a few short months later. The sea was calm but for the gentle lapping, as she circled her arms and legs to stay afloat. He turned his gaze away from her, keeping it instead on the water. But soon his panic returned and he shouted her name again. 'Claire, come back now, Claire!'

She backed away from the fish, splitting the shimmering school in half as she splashed and paddled toward the boat. And in that moment she was his Lasirèn, his long-haired, long-bodied brown goddess of the sea. With an angelic face like a bronzed Lady of Charity, Lasirèn was, it was believed, the last thing most fishermen saw before they died at sea, her arms the first thing they slipped into, even before their bodies hit the water. Like most fishermen he knew, Nozias, in his boat, next to his trap, net, hook, line, and tin can full of bait, kept a burlap sack in which he had a mirror, a comb, and conch shell, an amulet to attract Lasirèn's protection.

Even the regular hum of the sea seemed menacing until

his wife, swimming faster now, reached the boat. He leaned over and offered her his hand, and she took it and climbed back in, even as the twinkling fish and algae vanished, as though they had been only a mirage, returning the sea surface to an uninterrupted gray.

In his sloop, the water streaming down her body, his wife craned her neck to look up at Anthère Hill and its many large houses, their lights glowing in clusters in the distance. Above those houses, before Mòn Initil, was the Anthère lighthouse. Its stone tower was usually abandoned, but every once in a while, some young people, on a quest for adventure, would make their way to the steel door at its base, climb up the tower's winding staircase, and shine flashlights from its gallery, as if to duplicate its broken lamp. Tonight, it seemed, was one of those nights. Wiping the salt water from her face, Claire watched the flickering lights from the Anthère lighthouse, and then leaned toward Nozias.

'If it's a girl,' she said, 'Limyè Lanmè. Limyè Lanmè.' Sea Light. She cleared her throat and in a louder voice added, 'Claire like me. Then Limyè Lanmè. Claire of the Sea Light.'

'What if it's a boy?' he asked.

'Then Nozias, like you. Then Limyè Lanmè. Nozias of the Sea Light.'

He laughed at the ridiculous possibility of that name for a boy, but the girl name he liked a lot.

Now, on Claire's seventh birthday, up in the hills, in the gallery of the old lighthouse, there were once again lights. Some were flashlights. Some were hurricane lamps. But all of them were being lit, he knew, by young fishermen, as a tribute to Caleb, his friend.

Turning his eyes away from the lights, Nozias heard himself say to the fabric vendor, 'You will not change her name?'

The fabric vendor shook her head no.

'You will not let her ride motto taxis?'

'Non.' Both the woman's hands immediately rose to her chest, as though she had been struck there. 'I would never do that again,' she said.

Even after all these years of wooing the fabric vendor for Claire, he had never expected this to actually happen. But there was no turning back: from now on his Claire would be the fabric vendor's daughter.

'Before you leave Ville Rose,' the fabric vendor was saying, 'there are papers you must sign.'

'I had a letter written for her,' Nozias said. 'You can give it to her when she's older.'

'All right,' agreed the fabric vendor.

'Thank you,' he added, feeling the same unrelenting ache he sometimes felt standing at his wife's grave.

Nozias would later try to figure out where Claire got the courage to raise her skinny arms at that moment. He had underestimated her attachment to her few belongings and had assumed that she wouldn't want them in her new life. But at that moment, she raised her hand and pointed to the shack.

'Bagay yo,' she said, 'the things.' Not *her* things, but *the* things, as though she knew that nothing in the world was truly hers.

Nozias and the fabric vendor watched Claire make her way to the shack, weaving in and out of different groups of children, including the girls she had been playing with, and ignoring their attempts to catch her attention. From the time she had been returned to him at age three, Nozias had always been able to see her mother in her. Their lithe and limber bodies moved in the same way, their arms glued to their sides as they walked, their legs moving too slowly, languid from one step to the next. Nozias saw the girl pull open the wobbly door of the shack, then he turned away.

Claire did not have that many things, Nozias thought, only two navy-blue skirts and two white blouses for school, the pink birthday dress she was wearing and the one he'd had made before it, her nightdress, her notebook and reading primers, and the foam mattress and patchwork blanket with which she covered her cot, the one that had belonged to her mother. She wouldn't be able to carry everything by herself. The fabric vendor might not even want those things in her house. Gaëlle. The fabric vendor's name was Gaëlle. Now he could think it again. Now he could even say it. He could at least call her Madame Gaëlle. Madame Gaëlle Cadet Lavaud. His daughter was now Madame Gaëlle's daughter.

Madame Gaëlle was shifting the weight of her round frame from one fuzzy-slippered foot to another. She looked over at the two wooden steps one had to climb to enter the shack, then turned toward the dimming bonfire, where Caleb's wife, Josephine, was sitting, surrounded by her church friends.

Judging from the pattern of the stars in the sky, it was close to midnight. The lights from the hills had faded and the crowd was thinning out. The townspeople were drifting away, heading home. He felt sad that he had nothing more to say to this woman who was offering Claire a new life, this woman who from now on his daughter would call mother.

'How much is she bringing with her?' Madame Gaëlle now asked.

'I'll find her,' he said.

He felt her possibly judgmental stare on his back as he headed for the shack. He was doing his best not to keel over, but each time his feet became lodged in the sand, he was certain he would. But even before Nozias entered the shack, he sensed that Claire wasn't there. He pulled open the door; he was right. Her cot was covered with its usual blanket, untouched since she had tucked the corners under that morning. Hanging from a wire hanger on the wall were her school uniforms. On her pillow in a neat stack were her notebook and school primers.

His feet sure beneath him now, Nozias ran toward the water and called Claire's name. He then turned around and walked the dark trails between the shacks all the way to the entrance of the alley of coco de mer palms leading up to Anthère Hill.

Madame Gaëlle trailed behind him, joining him in the shouting of Claire's name. Others did too, walking off in different directions. Msye Sylvain and some of his children and grandchildren left the flaming clay oven of their bakery to also look for Claire. Msye Xavier, the boat builder, dropped his tools and followed the crowd. Madame Wilda, the net weaver, joined the search too. She, along with a group of others, walked to the edge of the water, looking for any sign of unusual movement.

When after some time Claire did not surface, many of Nozias's neighbors walked over to him and took turns telling him some variation of the idea that she had probably fallen asleep somewhere and would surely be home soon.

Caleb's wife, Josephine, came to embrace him. Her face was swollen from her many hours of crying, and the mourning scarf around her coarse black hair slid toward the back of her neck. Josephine was mute and suffered from elephantiasis in her right leg, which was double the size of her left leg. So Josephine moved slowly and spoke with her hands in a way that over the years Nozias and a few others who were close to Caleb had grown to understand. She touched her lips and mimed, 'Mèsi, thank you.' For what he wasn't sure. For spreading news of her husband's death among their neighbors? For witnessing the death itself?

Pounding both hands against her chest, she signaled 'kouraj, courage,' perhaps wishing it both for herself and for him.

As Josephine limped away from him, dragging the weight of her leg behind her, Nozias begged those heading to town to keep an eye out for his daughter. But inside of him was a new calm. He was certain that Claire would return, and he wanted to be there when she did.

Madame Gaëlle offered her white Mercedes. They could drive around town, looking for Claire, she said. But he was convinced that Claire hadn't gone too far, and he wanted his to be the first face she saw when she came back.

'I can't leave.' Madame Gaëlle reached over and squeezed his shoulder. 'She left because of me.'

She was probably right. Claire had never done anything like this before. Yes, she would sometimes go off walking, wandering around town, as her mother used to. But someone – if not him, then one of the women who kept an eye out for her – always knew in which direction she was headed, where she was going, and when she'd be back. But he felt it wouldn't be right to let Madame Gaëlle spend whatever time it would take Claire to return standing out on the beach. She also sensed his unease and suggested she wait in his shack.

'Don't worry, Nozias,' she said. 'Haven't I been here before?'

Madame Gaëlle's pearly gown now seemed as bright as the shiny side of the moon. She smelled like gardenias, like the gardenia-scented pomade the fishermen's wives who combed Claire's hair sometimes used to grease Claire's scalp. Madame Gaëlle walked in, just as she had the year before, when she'd come to see them. But this time she sat down on his cot. Her eyes were like two vacant pits, and in them he recognized a void that he could easily identify but could never soothe, not even in himself. She was there but not really. At one moment, her mouth opened and closed but nothing came out. She seemed to be recalling things she could not put into words.

He, though, was concentrating on his modest surroundings, on the way his cot caved in slightly under her weight. On the way the lamp was fluttering between shadow and light. Was it too hot in there? he wondered. Too cool? Too bright? Too dark? Her insistence on staying made him ashamed of his lack of comforts, of the smallness and feeble nature of his world.

'She will return, Madame,' he said. 'Excuse me.'

He backed out of the door, as though to show her his behind would be the height of disrespect. Then he left her alone in the shack and walked over to wait next to the rocks where the two of them had been sitting with Claire before Claire had disappeared.

The Frogs

Ten years before the night she showed up to take Nozias Faustin's child, Gaëlle Cadet Lavaud was expecting her own child. It was so hot in Ville Rose that year that dozens of frogs exploded. These frogs frightened not just the children who chased them into the rivers and creeks at dusk, or the parents who hastily pried the slimy carcasses from their young ones' fingers, but also twenty-five-year-old Gaëlle, who was more than six months pregnant and feared that, should the temperature continue to rise, she too might burst. The frogs had been dying for a few weeks, but Gaëlle hadn't noticed at first. They'd been dying so quietly that for each one that had expired, another had taken its place along the gulch near her house, each one looking exactly the same and fooling her, among others, into thinking that a normal cycle was occurring, that young was replacing old, and life replacing death, sometimes slowly and sometimes quickly. Just as it was for everything else.

After one sleepless night during which she'd been haunted by visions of frog carcasses slithering into her mouth and down her throat, Gaëlle had lingered under the mosquito net draped over their mahogany four-poster bed, as her husband, Laurent, slipped out of the room.

It was only after she heard the jingle of silverware in the dining room and her husband's effusive compliments to Inès, the housekeeper, about Inès's fried eggs and herring, that Gaëlle opened her eyes. But she didn't leave the bed until the engine of her husband's old Peugeot Cabriolet had been started, signaling that he was leaving for the fabric shop.

Soon after he was gone, she got up. Without changing out of her nightgown, she grabbed the ceramic chamber pot, which she kept by her bed. With the ever-vigilant Inès out of sight, Gaëlle walked out of the house and followed the almond grove that veered into a field of wild vetiver grass, then into a brook.

The sun had not been up for long, but it was already blazing in the middle of the sky. Still, the rocks and pebbles around the brook felt icy under Gaëlle's bare feet. She walked on them as she would a bed of dirt or grass, following the water's flow downstream until she spotted her first frogs. Just a few inches from the nearest lily pad, she noticed a green-horned frog that looked like a leaf with horns. Its legs were like a chicken's and it seemed to be almost frowning. Soon after, she found a brown dwarf jungle frog, which had the more ordinary look of a frog, except for what seemed like a long middle finger on its hind legs. The third was a tiny scarlet koki, whose melodious staccato song was believed to lull babies to sleep.

Gaëlle looked more closely. All three frogs, she saw, were dead, though of a more natural-seeming death than the frayed remains she'd seen in recent days. The three dead frogs were in crouching positions, as though frozen mid-jump or -crawl.

Rubbing her belly, she crouched down to pick up the frogs, then dropped them in the chamber pot. As she walked toward the base of a particular almond tree, where every day in the last week she'd performed a wordless burial for a handful of frog skins, she cradled the pot against her stomach. Most mornings when she'd reached the brook, she'd hoped to find at least one live frog, but carrying the dead frogs away made her feel useful, as though she were performing a crucial service that no one else would or could do. At times, it also felt like an extension of some of the childhood play she and her husband had relished as kids: the lizard burials in matchboxes, the butterfly and firefly trappings in glass jars. Though she vowed that each morning's brief hunt would be her last, she couldn't stop, so much had she convinced herself that the frogs needed her and she them.

She dug into the dew-softened dirt with her fingers, making a hole large enough to bury the frogs under the almond tree, then went back into the house and spent the day in bed. Some days, she felt so free that she hardly remembered the baby in her body at all. But on other days, days like today, she felt as though she were carrying a nest of snakes in her stomach. Inès brought her meals to her in bed on those days, but she barely ate anything: the breakfast of boiled plantains and fried eggs, the lunch of rice and beans, and the baby-fattening fried fish and stewed meats all looking to her even less appetizing than the dead frogs she'd planted in the ground.

'This heat and all this trouble with the frogs is surely a sign that something more terrible is going to happen,' Laurent told her when he came home that evening from town. He bent over to kiss her cheek, his face soaking with sweat.

Laurent Lavaud – Lolo to intimates, Lòl to his wife – was a small man, thinner and shorter than Gaëlle in her bare feet. He had a head of thick peppercorn hair and a wide grin that he seemed unable to restrain even when he was angry. He was from a family of tailors and textile shop owners, and because of the abundance of fabric at his own shop in town, dressed very well, lately favoring airy custom-made guayaberas and loose cotton pants.

While sliding into one of the two rocking chairs on the porch, Laurent told Gaëlle how when leaving Ville Rose's only radio station, WZOR, Radio Zòrèy or Ear Radio, where he sponsored programs and sometimes sat in the studio to listen to some broadcasts, he'd seen a group of young thugs hanging around the station entrance. Rubbing her belly with one hand, as had become a habit now, while fanning herself with a straw hat with the other, Gaëlle was only pretending to be listening when she said, 'Don't think about it, Lòl. It will ruin your appetite.'

He nodded, and then went back to talking about the frogs. 'In all my life, I've never heard of creatures dying like this.'

As an adolescent, Laurent had been a frequent hand-rolled-tobacco-leaf smoker. At times, when he made some pronouncement – for he had one of those voices that sounded as though it were always making pronouncements – he sounded a bit out of breath.

With their house in the middle of a notorious floodplain, near a tributary that joined several brooks, creeks, and rivers, Gaëlle thought that hundreds of rotting frogs might be an obvious catastrophe. But each morning, she made it a point to sniff the morning air and found no smell of dead frogs at all. As soon as their burnished skins and tiny organs were exposed to the sun, she realized, most of the frogs dried up, dissolving beneath the lily pads or into the riverbeds.

That there was no putrid odor was a lucky thing. At this stage of her pregnancy most things still sent Gaëlle retching. And yet two smells bothered her not at all: the clammy odor of dead frogs and the inky fragrance of brand-new cloth, which she enjoyed so much that at times her husband suspected her of secretly nibbling away at their merchandise whenever she was at their fabric shop.

A few weeks after they first began to die, the frogs and their cadavers disappeared altogether. The early-summer rains flooded the town's creeks and rivers, drowning the remaining frog population and depositing a tall layer of sandy loam near Gaëlle and Laurent's house. The waters had been strong enough to unearth the lengthy roots of the young vetiver grass that grew wild near their home. Some years they'd actually made a profit from their wild vetiver, which was not only good for the soil but also much sought after by two perfume company suppliers in the nearby southern city of Les Cayes. Those years when the vetiver flourished, Laurent and Gaëlle would use the extra money to plant a few more rows of almond trees near the outer sections of their property. Gaëlle especially loved the almond trees, and before she was pregnant and developed an aversion to them, would crush their fibrous fruits with river stones to dig out the kernels.

One evening, noticing that Laurent had returned late from the shop yet again, Inès, the bold and barrel-chested woman who'd been their housekeeper since they'd gotten married, greeted him with a silver tray and a glass of lemonade.

'Will Msye be eating tonight?' Inès asked in a scolding voice as deep as Laurent's.

Laurent shook his head no. He didn't like to eat at night and often arrived home late, after his wife had had her supper.

It had crossed Gaëlle's mind – as maybe it had Inès's – that since Gaëlle had known her husband since she was a girl and had become pregnant only a month into their marriage, he might have already taken up with another woman in town. Gaëlle also knew of his interest in the radio – his eagerness to watch the program hosts and hostesses work from the control booth was as strong as his erotic desires – and she believed him when he said that this was what he was doing in town after he closed the shop.

The next evening, Laurent came home early, carrying a handful of red azaleas for Gaëlle. Over the past few months, Gaëlle had learned that she could tolerate her husband's errors and obsessions, as long as they ended with red azaleas. There was comfort in that.

To escape the heat, they got in his Cabriolet and Laurent lowered the top and drove into the oldest part of town, past the vine-covered lookout tower of a castle that had been started in the years when Haiti was still a French colony, as a gift for Napoleon Bonaparte's sister Pauline. The castle, one of the town's most remarkable relics, had been left unfinished in 1802, when Pauline Bonaparte's husband died from yellow fever and she sailed with his body back to France. Some of its stone walls remained, although no one had seen fit to make any type of official monument out of them. Tubers were planted where Pauline's drawing rooms and boudoir should have stood. Cows and goats grazed around them. Children played afternoon soccer games in what would have been the zoological park meant to house Pauline's large menagerie of wild native animals.

Once they passed the ruins of the castle, which was called Abitasyon Pauline, Laurent drove over the old tracks behind the sugarcane fields and the umbrella-shaped roof of the kleren plant emerged. The smell of raw liquor filled the entire street; it was said that if you stood long enough on that street you could get drunk just from the air. Laurent and Gaëlle had tried it many times and it hadn't worked. They tried again that night to inhale some hazy happiness and forced lightheadedness, but it still didn't work. They then continued to the public lycée on the corner. The first floor was made of concrete and the second story was made of wood. Most of the structures in that part of town were built like this; construction materials were randomly mixed, creating a piecemeal that the people called achitekti pèpè.

Those drives, to her, were also journeys into their past. When they were students at this school, so few people had cars that dreaming about having one of your own was like wishing you had an airplane in your front yard. When Lòl was seventeen and his father bought him the black Peugeot Cabriolet they were still driving, he became the leader of their pack, the prince of their crowd. And she, being his intended, was the one scheduling the car, organizing trips, deciding who could or could not be a part of their inner circle. During the feast day of Sainte Rose de Lima, because roses were too expensive and she didn't like lilacs, they would cover the front of the car with red azaleas and she would sit next to him in the passenger seat as he drove in the religious procession with the car's top down.

They now drove farther uphill toward the old Anthère lighthouse, near where Gaëlle had spent her childhood.

They parked in front of the bougainvillea-covered gates of her grandparents' house, which had been empty since her mother and father had moved to Port-au-Prince. Looking down at the dark horizon over the beach, her husband reached for the flashlight on the dashboard and turned it on before they got out of the car. They followed a long and narrow footpath through the alley of palms that led down to the water. Hand in hand, they walked between the canoes and sailboats, most of which were named after saints, mothers, lovers, or wives. The flaps of many of the fishermen's windows were open, even at this late hour. Every few feet offered a glimpse of some private act by the light of a kerosene or hurricane lamp: a child being nursed or smacked, a husband and wife arguing, another pair undressing, a late supper of bread and tea being savored.

The fishermen's wives called out greetings to her and Laurent as they walked by. This was both the blessing and the curse of a town like theirs, a kind of village, really, to which Gaëlle and Laurent and their families had always belonged.

'Sea air's good for the baby,' many of the women called behind her.

The baby? What did they all know about the baby? Soon enough they would know everything, but for now the baby's story was only hers, Laurent's and hers.

Gaëlle hadn't wanted to do it. But because he claimed the fetus was developing too slowly, the gynecologist at Sainte Thérèse had insisted on a sonogram. The baby, determined

by the images to be a girl, was shown to have a cyst growing in her chest and down her entire spine. If she lived long
enough to be born, the doctor said, she would probably die
soon after. Both the doctor and Laurent had thought Gaëlle
should abort before she was too far along. But Gaëlle wanted
to carry full term, to see the whole thing through.

The next day Laurent had some other business in town and
asked Gaëlle if she could spend a few hours at the fabric
shop in his place. Gaëlle welcomed the idea. She relished the
thought of standing behind the counter and greeting customers, who'd offer her an excuse to roll out the massive
spools of muslin, kaliko, organza, and gabardine that lined
the shop's crowded shelves. All of this, she hoped, would also
keep her mind off the baby.

Gaëlle's first customer that morning was Claire Narcis,
a pretty young woman whose long, tightly cornrowed hair
sometimes made her look like a child.

After Gaëlle had become pregnant, Claire Narcis, like
almost everyone else, brought her a few small presents now
and then when she came into the shop. Most of the time it
was food, often fresh snapper, which Claire Narcis's man
had caught and which she would show Gaëlle in the shop
and then carry to Inès so it would be cooked fresh. Other
times it was mangoes, avocadoes, or yams. But every once
in a while, Claire Narcis would bring her something for
the baby, blankets or jumpers, neither pink nor blue, but

yellow or green, almost as a way of quietly inquiring about the sex of the child. This time, Claire Narcis brought an embroidered green blanket bordered in a delicate bridal lace that Gaëlle had sold her a week earlier without knowing its true purpose. That morning, with her pregnancy-sharpened sense of smell, Gaëlle could even detect on her the dead that Claire Narcis washed and dressed at Albert Vincent's funeral home most days. She caught a whiff of the embalming fluids and lemon-scented disinfectant and tried to ignore them as she untied her own shop's beige rope, unwrapped her own brown paper, to behold Claire Narcis's offering.

'I know it's bad luck to offer such a thing before the baby is here,' Claire Narcis began, lowering her gaze as people of a lesser station in life were expected to.

Gaëlle reached over the counter and raised Claire Narcis's face, rocking it gently in her palm. There was no time to say or do anything else. Other customers were walking through the gate, and although Gaëlle had two salespeople helping her, she was the only one Laurent trusted to collect payment.

'Thank you for everything you've given me,' Gaëlle told Claire Narcis, looking into her eyes. 'But no more.'

A gentle sheet of rain began to fall outside. As the sun dimmed and the air darkened and the sound of the rain grew louder and louder on the shop's tin roof, a group of soaked passersby entered the shop's front gallery and stood, packed next to one another, in the space between the counter and the door. They were quiet, strangely so, as the rain grew in intensity, pounding the dust into mud.

Gaëlle couldn't help but worry that the rivers near her house might swell again, bringing mudslides down from the hills. Hers and Laurent's was now the only house so close to the rivers. The other houses, newer yet shabbier, had been dragged downstream year after year in flash floods, many with entire families inside. Soon after they'd gotten engaged, Laurent had chosen the land and location as a surprise. He'd sketched the plans for the house himself and had spent his nights after work at the shop updating and revising each detail as the house was built from the ground up. He had driven to the capital to purchase the gables and louvers himself. (He had refused to get married until the house was done.) So now, after all that, he wasn't going to just pick up and move.

Many of the peasants living in the villages surrounding Ville Rose were just as stubborn. Laurent often held meetings in the shop with the peasants who lived up- and downriver from them, warning them that the rivers were swelling in response to the lack of trees, the land erosion, the dying topsoil.

'What do you want us to do, Msye Lavaud?' they'd ask him in return. 'Help us find something to replace the wood we need for charcoal and we will stop.'

Sometimes, in Laurent's attempts to get the villagers to stop cutting down trees, he'd reach for the basest of metaphors, the most melodramatic pleas.

'It's like killing a child,' he'd say.

'If I have to kill a tree child to save my child,' they'd reply, 'I'll do it, sou de chèz.'

And now, because of the town's and villagers' needs, her husband's dream house might soon be underwater. She and Laurent might wake up one night floating in their bed, might have to climb on top of their roof to wait for the current to die down. Silently pondering all this, Gaëlle put her hands on the back of her widening hips. Might she even have to give birth in a tree?

'It's terrible,' Claire Narcis declared in a now thunderous voice so that she'd be heard above all the others and above the pounding rain. 'With all the heat and rain this year, we'll either melt or be washed away,' she added, as though interpreting each layer of worry on Gaëlle's face.

Gaëlle continued to measure Claire's order, adding a few more yards as degi, in gratitude, and leaving it to the others taking shelter in the shop to continue the discussion.

'These frogs dying earlier this year weren't a good sign either.' Suzanne Boncy, the octogenarian florist and a Miss Haiti during the Second World War, was the only one participating in the discussion in French rather than Creole. All the voices now came booming out, almost deafening in the shop's small space, competing with hers.

'Not all bad the frogs died,' Elie, the town's best car mechanic butted in. 'Knew a crazy woman once. Would catch small frogs by the river, throw them in her mouth. Smaller and more colorful they are, more poison frogs have in them. Woman died from this, everyone said so. Better for the children and for crazy people the frogs are not around.'

Madame Boncy reached into the side pocket of her billowing pink dress and pulled out a folded copy of the town's one-page weekly newspaper. She pointed to a story about the dead frogs and, for those who couldn't read, explained erpétologie, or the study of reptiles and amphibians, including frogs. The article in the paper had been written by a herpetologist who had come all the way from Paris to uncover the reasons for the frogs' dying. According to Madame Boncy, the herpetologist had stated that, given his studies of the condition of the frog carcasses and the dirt and water samples he'd taken of their environment, and given the climate and blistering temperatures in Ville Rose that summer, the frogs had probably died from a fungal disease caused by the hotter-than-usual weather.

The rain was winding down, and soon it was sunny outside again. The people who'd come into the fabric shop to seek shelter were now making their way back into the street. The bells of Sainte Rose de Lima chimed the noon hour and the camions and other public transportation vehicles began circulating again, splashing muddy water everywhere.

'Mèsi, Claire,' Gaëlle said as she handed her the package.

Claire's eyes were once again lowered, her shoulders slouched. 'Fòk nou voye je youn sou lòt,' she said before walking out. 'We must look after each other.'

The next few mornings were dazzling, filled with splinters of daylight that, all over the house, crisscrossed the mahogany floors. These were the types of mornings – quiet, sun-soaked – that evaporated all of Gaëlle's fears about the outcome for the baby, even about living in the path of dangerous waters.

One of those mornings, a few weeks later, Gaëlle was planning to work with Laurent in the shop for the day and he was waiting for her in the car. She detested wearing muumuus, but at this point she had no choice.

The passenger seat had grown small for her as her belly had expanded. Though Laurent was already inside the car, looking pensively down the stone pathway leading toward the road, the passenger side door was locked. Before she was pregnant, she might have hopped over the open top, but no more.

He unlocked the door, then held out his hand and helped her squeeze her body into the seat. He reached back and placed his hand on her lap, tapping it gently, as was his habit, as though following a beat.

Before he could put the key in the ignition, she said, 'I want the baby to be named Rose.'

'For Sò Rose?' he asked.

She nodded.

Sò Rose, a direct ancestor of Gaëlle's, was the free colored woman, the wealthy affranchie, who'd founded the town after Pauline Bonaparte had left. Sò Rose herself had been named by her slave mother and French father after Sainte Rose de Lima, the patroness of the southern region.

Gaëlle wanted to tell her husband that, whether their

child was dead or alive, maimed or perfect, she would always love her. She loved that this child would connect them through time and that she would be born during their very first year of marriage. She wanted him to know that she couldn't bear the thought of being separated from this Rose sooner than she had to. Instead she said, 'It's a good name. Rose is a good name.'

'Common, though,' he said. 'She'll share it with so many. And then there's history.'

'A saint, a heroine, and a town. There's no shame in a name like that,' she said. 'She will carry it fine. It's a good name.'

Under normal circumstances, choosing a name – especially the name of their first child – would have been a glorious task, an occasion for those pleasant types of arguments that families discussed for years. He wanted this name, you often hear mothers say, and I wanted another. I won, or we compromised. But her husband wanted no name in this case. Whatever she'd proposed would have been okay with him, because he was convinced, just as the doctor was, that the child would not live even an hour, much less a day.

'Don't stay out too long tonight,' she said, covering his hands with hers on her lap.

'You're not coming to the shop?' he asked.

'Non,' she said.

She had been feeling some cramping in her lower back and down her legs, which had intensified since she'd sat down in the car. The baby was using her head to pound against Gaëlle's lungs and spine, and it didn't seem as though she'd stop anytime soon. At least she was still moving, Gaëlle thought.

'Should we call the doctor?' he asked.

'Not yet,' she said.

'Certain?'

'It's not so bad,' she said, and he seemed to believe her.

'Are you going to the radio station after closing?' she asked.

'Tomorrow is payroll,' he said. 'They're expecting me.'

'Why don't you have someone bring them the money?' she asked.

'I won't stay long,' he said, then kissed the side of her neck. It had thickened and grown darker as her due date approached, and part of her was eager to see it return to normal again: long and thin with a slight dusting of talcum powder.

She pressed her head against his so that his face could remain buried in her neck awhile longer.

'I have to go now if I'm coming home early,' he said, and turned away.

She opened the door and stepped out of the car. He got out and rushed to the other side, helping her to land on her feet, as the baby weight pulled her forward. She was grateful to remain upright as, after she repeatedly turned down his offer to walk her back into the house, she watched her husband get in the car and drive away. Standing there, watching him disappear behind the almond trees, she felt the muscles in her back tighten. She took slow, careful steps toward the house, then crawled into bed. She fell into a deep, exhausted sleep that was not even disrupted by Inès's occasional rumbling forays into the room to make sure she was all right.

When Gaëlle woke up, it was midafternoon and the pain in her body was gone, so she decided to go for a walk. A mound of stones had been brought down by a recent mudslide, turning the brook a deep brown. Some of the almond trees had prematurely shed their fruits and in many places her path was blocked by large branches.

Gaëlle stood on the edge of the brook and tried to imagine it filled, as it had been in better days, with crystalline water, rippling over the rocks. She imagined her husband and herself as teenagers, jumping in for summer-afternoon swims with their friends, splashing one another and muddying the flow in some spots. Then one of the regular afternoon drizzles would start, a sun shower, or ghost rain, as her husband and his friends – a year or two older and thus considerably wiser – liked to call it. The devil was beating his wife and marrying his daughter, they said. The drizzle was both the wife's and daughter's tears. The sun was God drying their tears.

Another sun shower was also starting that afternoon when Gaëlle saw a tiny red koki lodged between two rocks. It was a baby frog, smaller than the size of her pinky finger, and it was lying on its side covered in ants, its four tiny legs stiff and up in the air, as though it had made some effort to crawl away from the ants and had failed.

Squatting down, she picked it up, slapping the ants away. They scattered madly, while others crawled up and down her arms, stinging her. The ants must have not been there for long, because the koki was still whole, its interior organs, which she could spy through its sheer skin, intact. Without thinking, she wiped a warm mist from her face and stuffed the koki into her mouth.

The frog stank of mold and decay and was slippery as it landed on her tongue. And though the koki was dead, she imagined it struggling as she pushed back her head and allowed it to reach her throat. Among the many dreadful, difficult things about her pregnancy, after the doctor's dire verdict, was that she had grown to hate the smell of her own body. Most days she thought she smelled like a latrine. The very air that floated around her disgusted her. And sometimes, even though she had decided to keep it, the child growing inside of her repulsed her too.

Her body tried to resist the koki in her throat, her gullet forcing it back upward, nearly making her vomit. She took another vigorous gulp and forced it down farther until she could almost feel it land, somewhere deep inside of her.

Here they were, she thought, drawing the thought out in her mind. Two types of animals were now inside of her, in peril: her daughter, Rose, and now this frog. Let them fight it out and see who will win.

The sun shower ended and the sun peeked out brighter than before as she walked back to the house. She stopped walking now and then to fight the stirring in her belly, swallowing hard to dilute the bitter taste in her mouth. When she returned home, she was smiling more than she had for days.

'I was just going to come after you,' Laurent said, rushing to greet her at their front door. 'Inès told me you weren't feeling well. Did she prescribe rain?'

He was smiling his crooked smile. She was happy that he was smiling, but she was also happy that he had listened. He had come home early just as she'd requested. When he asked where she had been, she said, 'Avec les grenouilles. Par le ruisseau. La douche solaire.'

With the frogs, by the stream, when the sun shower began, had been a good enough explanation for him. She needed to walk to help the baby drop, to make easier the labor that lay ahead, possibly in a few short days, she said. That's why she walked to the brook every morning and sometimes in the afternoons too. He now understood that.

'But no more in the rain,' he said.

'It was not rain. It was a sun shower,' she said. But he no longer seemed to think there was a difference.

Her stomach now settled, she changed muumuus and that evening ate more of her cornmeal porridge supper than she had of anything else in weeks. She'd marveled at her own peaks of joy followed by self-pity, over the full course of her pregnancy. These dark moods, almost like strange premonitions, were normal, given the circumstances, the doctor had told her when she'd found it hard to trust that she and Laurent wouldn't also die along with the baby.

'After we survive this, no matter what happens to the baby, our obituaries in *La Rosette* will say that we died after a valiant battle with a long illness,' Laurent would try to comfort her by saying. 'We have many babies in us still.'

The following evening, the evening Gaëlle and Laurent's daughter, Rose, was born, was a clear and bright night with a full moon and a cloudless sky, crammed with stars. On one side of Gaëlle's room was a giant mirror and a lamp, both powered by the loud hum of the house generator. Seeing her half-naked body in the mirror at the foot of the bed made Gaëlle think of a jellyfish whose hood was billowing onto itself. Having the mirror there was originally her idea. She wanted to see her daughter as soon as she emerged from her body. She did not want to miss a second of looking into her child's face. But in the end, she changed her mind right before she began pushing, and she motioned for Inès to place a sheet over the mirror, just as one would after a death. She also refused to have either her husband or the doctor called.

'They are going to take her away from me,' she kept saying. Folding her body in two to push the baby out, Gaëlle felt flattened and weak one second and invincible the next. Soon after Inès reached down between her legs and pulled out her daughter, Gaëlle cut the umbilical cord herself with a pair of brand-new scissors from the shop.

Both Gaëlle and Inès wept at the child's swift arrival, but most of all at her unexpected flawlessness, at how magnificently whole she looked. She was plump and gorgeous, a swirl of tiny curls covering her perfectly round head. She let out a long wail when her bottom was slapped. Her arms flailed in the air with gusto. There were no cysts on her back, or anywhere else on her body.

She was perfect, a perfect little Rose, who nonetheless looked like her father. It was obvious that she would not grow up to be a tall or stately woman, but soon after her umbilical cord was clamped, her dark eyes were already open, and when her mother held her up to her breasts, she immediately opened her still blood-tinted little mouth and started nursing.

On that perfectly starry night, Laurent Lavaud did not make it home in time to meet his daughter, Rose. There had been a shooting at Radio Zòrèy, where, not knowing that his wife had begun her labor, he'd stopped for a minute to drop off more sponsorship money. The shots had rung out as Laurent was leaving the station, and he was struck by three bullets to the heart and died on the spot. Even before his body was cold and the pool of blood under it had been covered with limestone powder, people immediately began to declare that his shooting was related to a new, urgent plague in Ville Rose, one that was even deadlier than the frogs: gangs.

Ghosts

BERNARD DORIEN WAS LIVING in Cité Pendue, a destitute and treacherous extension of Ville Rose. Some people called it the region's first circle of hell.

In spite of its stark reputation, Cité Pendue – twenty-eight miles from Port-au-Prince and eight miles from the center of Ville Rose – was actually only a midlevel slum. After all, it had a few Protestant churches, many Vodou temples, some restaurants and bakeries, and even a couple of dry cleaners.

For a while, there were no gang wars, just one gang, whose headquarters was a former food-storage warehouse that the dozen or so young male inhabitants called Baz Benin. (The men of Baz Benin gave themselves the monikers of Nubian royalty, which also happened to suggest menacing acts in Creole – Piye, for example, meaning 'to pillage,' Tiye, meaning 'to kill.')

Bernard's parents were restaurateurs in Cité Pendue. They had a slightly larger yard on their pebbled street than most of their neighbors, so they'd closed it off with corrugated metal, and there they served at least thirty customers per night, more if the turnover was fast. At the center of their business were four long wooden tables spread out beneath a string of generator-fueled lightbulbs. They sold rice and beans, plantains, and cornmeal, but their specialty was barbecued pigeon meat.

The place was called Bè, Bernard's parents' nickname for him. Bè also meant 'butter,' and Bernard's mother liked to say when everyone asked her how she was doing that she was churning butter from water – m ap bat dlo pou m fè bè – which meant that she was always attempting the impossible, trying to make something worthwhile out of little or nothing.

Bernard's parents had moved to Cité Pendue from a village in the surrounding mountains at a time when Cité Pendue was being used by most people as a temporary perch while their peasant children finished primary school. But as the trees in theirs and other provinces vanished into charcoal and the mountains crumbled and gave way, washing much-needed topsoil into the sea, the Doriens stayed in Cité Pendue, much as their neighbors had to, and raised their son – and hundreds of pigeons that over the years they sold both alive and dead for breeding or for food.

Most of their customers at one point had been nervous young men who wanted to perform a Cité Pendue ritual before their first sexual encounter. They'd slit a squab's throat, then let it bleed into a mixture of Carnation condensed milk and a carbonated malt beverage called Malta. Sometimes their fathers would come with them and, after the sons had held their noses and forced down the drink, the fathers would laugh and say, as the pigeon's headless body gyrated on the ground, 'I pity that girl.'

It was a ritual Bernard's parents didn't approve of. But for each bird that was killed this way they were paid enough to breed more. They mourned the days when people had come to buy pigeons for racing, or to train as carriers, or as pets for their small children. Then they began missing the days of the fathers and sons, because suddenly their customers were beefy young men who'd gathered themselves into what were at first called 'popular organizations,' then gangs.

The gang members were also called chimè, chimeras or ghosts, and were, for the most part, street children who couldn't remember ever having lived in a house, boys whose parents had been murdered or had fallen to some deadly disease, leaving them alone in the world. Later, these young men were joined by older neighborhood men. These older men were 'connected' – that is, ambitious business owners as well as local politicians used them to swell the ranks of political demonstrations, gave them guns to shoot when a crisis was needed, and withdrew them when calm was required.

Sometimes, before one of these demonstrations, so many men came for the milk-Malta-pigeon-blood mix that Bernard's parents were tempted to close the pigeon-killing business for good. And finally they did.

Still, with the money they'd made from the pigeons, the Doriens were able to add to the menu. They bought the house next door to them, the one attached to the Baz Benin

warehouse, and added a few more tables to serve their growing clientele. Bernard's father also bought a small camion
that he drove back and forth between Cité Pendue and Ville
Rose daily, packed with people and sometimes livestock. He
was always at the restaurant for their busiest time, though,
between nine in the evening and one in the morning, when
the gang members, many of whom had brought the drug
trade with them from the capital, would take over most of
the establishment. Watching these boys drift from being
mere sellers to casual users of what they liked to call the
poud blan, the white man's powder, watching these boys
grow unrecognizable to anyone but one another, Bernard's
parents were repulsed and afraid. But they still kept the
place open, because the same blight that was destroying Cité
Pendue was allowing them to prosper, to send their son to
school with the heirs and heiresses of Ville Rose's tiny middle class, to make contacts that one day might help him get
a good job or find a decent match for marriage.

To stay out of the gangs, Bernard had joined the regular
national police force (not the Special Forces). Although he
was just twenty years old, scrawny, and had the distinctive
family trait of a disproportionately large head that gained
him the nickname Tèt Veritab, Breadfruit Head, the police
academy in Port-au-Prince had accepted him. But Bernard
had found that, even though his training was in the capital,
he couldn't be a police rookie and have his parents survive in
Cité Pendue. Every time a gang member was arrested in Cité
Pendue, Bernard was blamed for it, putting his parents' lives

in danger. More than this, his parents were heartbroken that he had left. His mother told him every time they spoke on the phone how she wished he'd return home. It was his first nearly fatal asthma attack in some time – he'd suffered from them since childhood – that forced the police academy to let him go during a particularly taxing training session. But while he'd been in Port-au-Prince, spending endless hours in traffic, in tap taps, communal buses, and taxis, he'd fallen in love with the radio, especially the news and commentary, call-in, and interview programs, which seemed to blast from every house, car, street-corner business, or shop. So now Bernard spent all the time he wasn't helping out at his parents' restaurant working as a modestly paid newswriter at Ville Rose's only radio station, Radio Zòrèy.

Having grown up in Cité Pendue, and having seen many of the changes there firsthand, Bernard imagined himself becoming the kind of radio journalist who'd talk about what he preferred to call the 'geto,' from the inside. An idea came to him one night while he was walking from his parents' small concrete-block kitchen, which they had built close to the street to tempt passersby with appetizing smells, to the table where Tiye, a one-armed gang leader, was nursing a beer and a massive cigar. Tiye was wearing his plastic-steel-combination artificial arm under a long-sleeved peacock-blue shirt and was expertly raising and lowering the beer to his mouth with the prosthetic's shiny metal hooks. Surrounded by three eager 'lieutenants,' Tiye was laughing so hard about the way he'd once slapped a man, when he had both his arms – sandwiching the man's head between his palms and pounding both his ears – that he had to dab tears from his own cheeks. Bernard, eavesdropping, wished he'd had a video camera, or at least a tape recorder. He wanted the rest of Cité Pendue, the rest of Ville Rose, the rest of the country, to know what made men who were the same age as he, men who lived in the same place he did, men like Tiye, cry.

We can't move forward as a neighborhood, as a town, or as a country – he'd thought as he brought Tiye and his friends another round of beers – unless we know what makes these men cry. They cannot remain chimè, chimeras, phantoms, or ghosts to us forever. His commentary segment at Radio Zòrèy, if he were ever given one, would be called *Chimè*, or *Ghosts*.

His only viable competition at the station would be a popular weekly program called *Di Mwen*, or *Tell Me*, a weekly interview/gossip show, hosted by a raspy-voiced woman named Louise George. Just as *Di Mwen* had been at first, *Ghosts* would be controversial, but soon people all over Ville Rose would tune in to it – Bernard was certain of it. A kind of sick voyeurism would keep them listening, weekly, monthly, however often he was on. People would rearrange their schedules around it. They wouldn't be able to stop themselves from discussing it. What are the men and women in the geto up to now? listeners would ask themselves. They'd be encouraged to figure out ways to alleviate the gang problem. Also featured on the program would be psychologists, human-behavior experts, and neighborhood planners.

Max Ardin, Jr., who was Bernard's friend and the host of a rap music program at the station, liked Bernard's pitch. But he was also skeptical. Though he was only nineteen and had gotten the job through his father's connections, Max Junior still knew a lot about the radio business. Besides, Bernard trusted him.

'I'm feeling everything you're saying, but the management won't buy it,' Max Junior said while keeping Bernard company one afternoon as Bernard typed away on an old electric typewriter at the far end of a long desk in the newsroom. 'Who'll sponsor a program like that?'

'The government should sponsor it,' Bernard said, as he retyped that day's news from the wires into conversational Creole for the announcer to read on the air. 'We'd be offering a public service.'

'You should pitch it to our boss,' Max Junior said. 'But I bet he'll be too scared to take it on.'

Just as his friend predicted, Bernard's program was not picked up, at least not with his involvement. But a few weeks later, while typing that afternoon's news script, Bernard heard a taping for a program called *Homme à Homme,* or *Man to Man.* The program, announced the host, a former army colonel, would consist of in-studio conversations between gang members and Cité Pendue and Ville Rose business leaders.

'They'll hash out their differences,' he heard the colonel say, 'with the help of a trained arbitrator.'

The first program did just that, pairing an ice factory owner, who'd had his place broken into at least once a month for over a year, with another gang leader from Cité Pendue, a nemesis of Tiye's, who was believed to have vandalized the ice factory.

'What do you expect?' the gang member told the ice vendor. 'You're chilling in all this ice while we're here boiling in hell.'

The arbitrator, a female psychologist, who'd called in to the station from Port-au-Prince, then suggested the obvious, that the businessman find some way to share his ice, sell it at a lower price to the people who lived near his factory, and that the gang leader respect the property of others.

What's worse, Bernard was forced to hear the entire show again on the radio his mother sometimes had on in the restaurant, as he was serving drinks to Tiye and his crew, among others. Tiye and his friends had known about Bernard's pitch for the show – he had approached them as possible guests – and, as he served them their beers, they teased him. 'Hey, man, they stole your idea!'

A few of them tried to grab Bernard as he put the bottles on the table – as if to squeeze out the anger they knew was bubbling inside him. The more they laughed, the angrier he got. Tiye was still laughing when he said, 'Bernard, bro, that show is kaka. I should find them all and kick their ass.'

'That's right,' Piye, Tiye's second lieutenant, chimed in.

'Bernard,' someone else said. 'You should kick the ass of the guy who stole your show.'

Just then Bernard's mother called him over to the kitchen, to pick up more beers, he thought. But on top of the old refrigerator in which they kept the drinks was his mother's most lavish personal acquisition, an old rotary phone. His friend Max Junior was on the line.

He thought Max Junior would be calling about the show, but instead his friend said, 'I'm calling to say good-bye, man. My fucking father is sending me to Miami.'

'Really?' Bernard said, both incredulous and sad. 'When are you coming back?'

'I don't know,' his friend replied.

'Who's doing your show while you're gone?' Bernard asked.

'I'm not sure,' Max Junior said.

'Maybe I can fill in for you,' Bernard said.

'Maybe,' Max Junior said, then added, 'Man, they stole your idea.'

'Truth is, *Homme à Homme* is not the show I wanted to do,' Bernard said, trying to contain his sadness over both his departing friend and his show. 'I wanted something closer to the skin. Something more personal.'

Tiye and his guys were chanting from their tables, 'Kraze bouda yo! Kraze bouda yo! Kick their asses! Kick their asses!' Their voices were so loud that Bernard could barely hear Max Junior anymore.

'I'll call you from Miami,' Max Junior said.

After he hung up, Bernard stood with his head pressed against the concrete wall and waited for Tiye and his crew to leave before returning to the tables. His mother and the neighborhood girls she'd hired came in soon after to wash the dirty dishes. His mother's stern expression never changed. It was as if the heat of the kitchen had melted and sealed it. He thought, miserably, that even if she didn't work again for the rest of her life, whatever beauty she'd had when she was young and wasn't cooking for dozens of people every day would never come back.

He convinced his mother to go to sleep a little earlier than usual, before going to bed himself. In his room, whose walls and ceiling he'd painted bright red when he was a teenager, he felt both Max Junior's sudden good-bye and the loss of the show deep in his gut. Now it would be much harder to pitch his idea to another radio station in the capital or somewhere else. The programmers could always say, 'But *Homme à Homme* is already airing. We don't want to give these gangsters too much of a platform.' He fell asleep thinking he'd have to redefine his idea, sharpen it, add music. When he came back from Miami, Max Junior could help him with that. They could play reggae-influenced hip-hop like Max Junior played on his show, while in between songs Bernard would let his neighbors speak.

Bernard was still asleep the next morning when a dozen Special Forces policemen dressed all in black and with balaclava-covered faces knocked down the front gate of his parents' house, climbed up to his room, and dragged him out of bed. He was shoved into the back of a pickup even as his mother wailed uncontrollably and his father shouted that a great injustice was taking place.

When they reached the nearest commissariat, a small crowd of print, TV, and radio journalists, including his boss, were waiting for him. The night before, Ville Rose's police spokesperson, a shrill-voiced woman, explained, there had been a shooting at Radio Zòrèy. Four men with M16s and machine guns had been seen jumping out of an SUV. They had shot at the front gates of the two-story building, killing Laurent 'Lolo' Lavaud, a fabric shop owner and very generous Radio Zòrèy sponsor. The police had arrested Tiye, the notorious head of Baz Benin. Tiye had named Bernard as the auteur intellectuel, the mastermind, of the crime, the person who had sent him and his men to do the job. Bernard was not allowed to speak. He was only meant to stand there, like a menacing prop, surrounded by the hooded police team with his wrists handcuffed behind his back, while the same flashbulbs kept erupting and a video camera light pierced his eyes and questions were shouted at his accusers.

The box of a room where Bernard was then taken to be questioned was narrow and hot, with the stench of fresh vomit wafting in the air. In addition to the creaking metal chair, on which he was placed with his hands still cuffed behind him, the room had a cement floor and a ceiling light box whose flickering beams streamed past the black cloth that one of the policemen had placed over Bernard's eyes.

During his questioning by the police, Bernard was repeatedly punched on the back of his head. This reminded him of Tiye's description of the two-handed slaps given to the men who'd once been hit by Tiye's lost arm.

'You know Tiye?' Because of the blindfold, which also covered his ears, many of the voices sounded distant and distorted, until some of the officers moved their mouths close to his ears and began shouting so loud that he thought his eardrums would pop. One of them blew smoke into his face. In his brief police training, Bernard had not yet gotten to the classes on suspect interrogation methods. Were these the methods they would have covered? he wondered bitterly.

'Wi,' Bernard replied, coughing. 'I know Tiye.' His lungs felt as though they were closing in a new way, as though they would never open again. The constriction forced out chunks of last night's dinner onto the front of his pajama top, and when he was allowed to bend his neck, down on his lap.

'How you know Tiye?' The questions continued, sometimes from two or three mouths yelling in a deafening chorus in each of his ears.

'Lives in my neighborhood . . . He comes . . . He eats at my parents' restaurant,' he stammered.

'You're a big man, uh? Your parents have a restaurant in the slums. I'm hungry now. Feed me. Feed me,' one of the officers shouted.

The others were laughing even as Bernard hiccupped. To his now burning ear, there was no difference between their laughter, their taunting, and that of Tiye and his crew. They could all have switched places and no one would have noticed.

'How much did you pay the crew from Baz Benin to shoot at the station?' another officer yelled.

'Nothing . . . I . . .'

'So they did it for free?'

'Non . . .'

'You paid?'

'Non . . .'

'Which is it?'

'No involvement . . .'

'You trained with the police for a while, didn't you, so you could become a big-shot criminal?'

They threw some ice water on his face and laughed some more. Panicked, he tried to rise from the chair, but someone shoved him back down. With the smoke and the vomit and the cold water, he felt as though he were drowning.

After the questioning, Bernard was left alone in the dank cell, still blindfolded and shackled. That afternoon, his mother and father came to see him. They were allowed to remove the strip over his eyes before kneeling down on the floor to get closer to him. His mother was quietly weeping over his body, which was curled up in a fetal position.

'Bè, could you have done such a thing?' his father asked. Bernard's father sounded at once worried and stern, and even more distraught about scolding his son. An old facial tic, the quick batting of his eyes and involuntary twitching of his mouth, had returned to Bernard's father's face. Bernard had not seen it in such a long time that he'd almost forgotten it.

Bernard shook his head no.

'I did nothing, Papa,' he said, his throat aching as he tasted the chunks of vomit still lingering in his mouth. His father, he knew, needed a denial from him in order to proceed full-force with his fight.

His mother reached into her bra and handed him an inhaler. 'Bè,' his mother said breathlessly, as though she were having an attack herself, 'we had to pay extra to bring this in to you.'

'They're not beating me too bad,' he mumbled. 'Not yet anyway. You see I have no blood on me.'

The mother raised his filthy pajama top, covered with vomit and sweat, to look for cuts, wounds.

'The lawyer we got for you,' his father said, 'her cousin is a magistrate. She says she's going to try to move things quickly, in your favor.' Somehow his father's mouth now remained a controlled line. 'You might have to go to the pénitencier in Port-au-Prince, until we get you out.'

They'd talked to Tiye's second lieutenant, Piye, a few hours before, his father told him. His father had told Piye that Bernard would have never asked Tiye to kill anyone. Piye had told his parents to stay calm. The case was a lamayòt, a vapor, he said. Nothing was going to stick. Give it a few more hours. Let it cool off.

With his father's help, Bernard pulled himself up. Had they called his radio colleague and friend Max Junior? he asked. Max Junior was supposed to leave for Miami, but might still be in town. He too might have some helpful contacts.

He'd tried to see Max Junior at his home, his father said, but was told by Max's father that his son had left the country.

Bernard raised both his hands to his face and began sobbing. Neither of his parents could remember seeing him cry like this before, not as a grown man. His body was shaking, the hopelessness sinking in. In spite of having his parents' arms around him, he felt deserted and alone.

But it turned out that, in fact, he was actually on a fast track. An hour or so after his parents left, a black-robed magistrate came into Bernard's cell – an exception to his having to go before a judge weeks and months or even years after being put in jail – and informed him of the charges against him. He was not only considered the mastermind of the radio station shooting, but was said to be a turncoat police rookie. Bernard feared that he'd rot in an overcrowded jail cell at the pénitencier in the capital or be disappeared before he even got there. He began plotting ways to get his story out. He would write something for the radio, for Radio Zòrèy. But would the people who ran Radio Zòrèy and the people who listened to it even want to hear his side of the story?

That same evening, in the interrogation cell, having slept

through the dinner hour, as Bernard lay there with his face pressed against a particularly cool and hollow groove on the floor, he saw a line of black shiny boots march toward him. He was blindfolded once again, then thrown into what felt like the backseat of a car. He was shoved out on the street in front of his parents' restaurant, still blindfolded, at around 10 p.m.

After his own arrest, Tiye had made a deal. As head of Baz Benin, Tiye had collected drug-related dirt on everyone, from the lowest policeman in Cité Pendue to a few of the area's judges. And now he'd talked to the police and exchanged his slew of records, including records of bank deposits for bribes, for both his and Bernard's freedom.

Later that evening, bathed and clean, Bernard was lying on his bed in his red room, staring at the crimson ceiling. He had called Max Junior's home and asked for him, and after he said his name, Max Junior's father – Max Senior – had slammed down the phone on him. That's when he began writing.

Yes, he'd write something for the radio, a report that would contain all the details of the experience he had just been through. He would make it clipped and fast, like a story told out of breath, but since he would no longer have his own radio program, or even sit in for Max Junior, he would have someone else narrate it for him. He would, if he could convince her, get Louise George, the hostess of *Di Mwen*, to read his story on the air. He could imagine her not interviewing anyone else the week she'd read it. His story, read in her signature down-tempo, yet passionately hoarse voice, would, along with the many sponsor spots and commercial announcements that only she was able to get, fill the entire hour of her show. Her boss, the owner of the station, would probably not want her to do it, but, ballsy as ever, she would threaten to quit if he stopped her, and since hers was the most popular show on Radio Zòrèy, she would prevail. She would begin her program in the usual way that evening, as though he were actually sitting across from her inside the studio, at the radio station, from which he was now surely banned.

'Tell me, Bernard Dorien,' she would say to the empty studio chair. 'We need to hear your story.' And then she would read his story and explain why he wouldn't be there to talk to them directly about his experience.

But soon his parents interrupted his writing and fantasizing. They hovered over him, leaning over his bed as his mother handed him a hot cup of verbena tea to further calm his nerves.

Even though his mother hadn't cooked, so as to discourage her regular customers from coming, people had still stopped by for drinks, and to express their relief and offer their congratulations about his release. His parents were also here to tell him that Msye Tiye was downstairs and wanted to see him.

Bernard handed the teacup, still full, back to his mother,

then raised the edge of his mattress and placed his notebook under it, on the metal spring.

'Down soon,' he said.

'Don't be tardy,' his mother said, as though he were about to be late for school.

His parents filed out dutifully, one after the other, their bodies tense with a new level of worry.

In the yard, Tiye and the lieutenants were already settled at a table with drinks.

'No need to pay tonight,' Bernard's father said, before joining his mother in the kitchen.

Tiye had a few more guys with him now for extra protection. These men listened with rapt attention as Tiye described some of what he'd just been through. 'I thought they were going to jack me up real bad,' he was saying. 'Real bad.'

Bernard could hear Tiye's slow and severe voice grow louder, drumming like the policemen's voices, deep inside his head, as he walked over to Tiye's table.

Tiye said: 'You know how they take some of the guys to Port-au-Prince and you don't never hear from them again. Or how they just beat the shit out of you. Then yeah, I thought I was done, fini.'

He said all this casually, almost matter-of-factly, with a kind of amused air, which indicated that, if this had happened, it wouldn't have been a big deal. This was how Tiye and his guys faced the inevitable, Bernard thought.

Crossing the yard on shaky legs, Bernard realized that this was all a game to Tiye. He had turned Bernard in, then rescued him, and now he was having a few laughs and some beers. It was all in a day's work. Still, Bernard couldn't shake the feeling that one day they would all be shot. Like the fabric shop owner Laurent Lavaud and like almost every young man living in the slums. One day it might occur to someone, someone angry and powerful, and maniacal – a police chief or a gang leader, or a leader of the nation – that they, and all those who lived near or like them, would be better off dead.

Bernard walked over to Tiye's table and held out a hand to him. Pounding his fist on his chest, near his heart, in greeting, Tiye said, 'No hard feelings?' Then Bernard noticed that Tiye's gums were as red as the walls of his room, as though he had a perpetual infection or had been eating raw meat.

'Did they jack you up?' Tiye asked Bernard.

'Wasn't so bad,' Bernard said.

Tiye wasn't wearing his prosthetic arm and the sleeve of his shirt sagged. With his good hand, Tiye motioned for the guy who was sitting next to him to get up so Bernard could sit down.

Bernard looked more closely at the space where Tiye's missing arm would have been. He thought he saw something white, as though a polished piece of bone were protruding from under thinly scarred skin. He tilted his head to see it better, while trying not to seem obvious. For a flash of a moment, Bernard looked over his own body to see if anything of his was gone.

The restaurant was unusually full for the hour. Above the din of voices requesting drinks, Bernard could hear people asking his parents whether it was true that he had been released, then walking by the table where he was sitting with Tiye to see for themselves. Some even shook his hand, a few women kissing him on the cheek.

He was now a kind of everyman hero, someone who had seen the bowels of hell and returned.

He now imagined beginning his own radio program with a segment on lost limbs. Not just Tiye's, but other people's as well. He would open *Chimè* with a discussion of how many people in Cité Pendue had lost arms, legs, or hands. He would go from limbs to souls – to the number of people who had lost siblings, parents, children, and friends. These were the real ghosts, he would say, the phantom limbs, phantom minds, phantom loves that haunted them because they were used, then abandoned, because they were out of choices, because they were poor.

It was nearing closing time. His mother brought the final beers to the table. She avoided their eyes as she lifted the bottles from her tray and put them down. Bernard waited for her to return to the kitchen before raising his drink toward Tiye and clinking the top of his bottle with his. Tiye's bottle struck his with force. Bernard saw a brief spark, and the top of his bottle broke apart, leaving a jagged gap in the glass. A shard landed on the table with a splash of beer; another fell to the clay floor.

Tiye laughed, a loud, haunting laugh that reminded Bernard of the officers at the prison, a laugh that flashed his crimson gums as he pointed his beer bottle in Bernard's direction. 'If you're doing a little piece on the radio,' he said, 'can't be some homo masisi bullshit like that *Homme à Homme*. Needs to be real.'

Tiye stopped laughing, then filled his mouth with beer, swishing it around loudly, as if he were gargling.

'Don't worry,' he said to Bernard, but also, it seemed, to himself. 'As long as I'm here, nothing will happen to us tonight.'

The next morning, Bernard Dorien was found dead in the bed of his red bedroom. He had been murdered in the same way that Laurent Lavaud, the owner of the fabric shop, had, with three bullets expertly, and, in Bernard's case, silently, administered to his heart.

The restaurant had already opened for breakfast when his parents found him, so the neighborhood girls continued to serve the food they'd cooked, as a Cité Pendue magistrate and an anti-gang prosecutor came and wrote up their reports.

'An eye for an eye. Another bandit has been erased from the face of this earth,' began Radio Zòrèy's morning newsflash. It was a piece that, were he still alive and working there, Bernard Dorien might have been assigned to write.

Home

MAX ARDIN, JR.'S GIRLFRIEND was missing. Crowding his father's vast ring-shaped living room were the hundred or so guests who'd come to greet him on the first night of his first visit home in ten years.

On the phone from Miami, Max Junior had told his father, Max Senior, that he was coming home with a girl.

'What kind of girl is she?' Max Senior had asked.

'Just a girl,' Max Junior had said.

'What family?' Max Senior insisted, hoping his son would rattle off the cognomen of one from their milieu, from Miami or the capital or some other respectable town. But instead Max Junior had replied in jest, 'The human family,' causing his father to confess that he was worried Max Junior was bringing home a poor foreigner.

'She's Haitian and she knows where Ville Rose is,' Max Junior said, in an attempt to console his father.

'Mon Dieu.' Max Senior feigned a gasp, then laughed. 'A poor blan who's also Haitian and knows where Ville Rose is.'

From the lowest step of the old rosewood staircase, which had been buffed and shined back to life for the special evening, Max Junior now scanned his father's book-lined living room for familiar faces. He spotted two of his father's oldest friends, Suzanne Boncy, ageless beauty queen, and Albert Vincent, the town's funeral director and now also its mayor. Around Suzanne Boncy were a slew of other aging beauties, most of whom had too much rouge streaked across their cheeks, and the one or two representatives from the other group of his father's friends that Max now found most bearable, the children of these women and their Ville Rose men, the Canadian-, French-, Mexican-, or U.S.-educated sons and daughters, who preferred the capital, but made the occasional quick trip to Ville Rose to check on their parents.

Before he'd left Ville Rose ten years ago, Max Junior had spent countless afternoons and evenings in the company of leaner, more attractive versions of these people. He had attended birthdays, weddings, and funerals, watched soccer matches, and played epic games of cards and dominoes after countless Sunday dinners. Aside from the children in his school and the occasional girlfriends he was rumored to have, these were the only kinds of people whose company his father enjoyed.

Things had been different when Max Junior was younger. Before his mother had divorced his father and moved to Miami, Max Senior had taken the time to attend conferences and lectures with Max Junior and his mother at the Alliance Française or the foreign embassies in Port-au-Prince. By the time he was nineteen, and his mother had left, Max Junior had already completed his primary- and secondary-school studies and had also gotten a U.S. mail-order bachelor's degree in education. He had attended École Ardin for primaire; once he was too old for the school, his father had become his sole instructor.

It had always been Max Senior's dream to have his son help him run his school. But at nineteen years old, Max Junior wanted to be a radio deejay. So Max Senior used his connections to help, arranging for his son to host his own program on Radio Zòrèy. Max Senior had also encouraged his son to continue his studies in Miami. He'd never lost the hope that one day Max Junior would return and take over École Ardin. But instead Max Junior chose to stay in Florida, to manage the sandwich shop his mother had opened in Miami's Little Haiti neighborhood.

Max Junior had met Jessamine at the sandwich shop, where she'd come to interview for a part-time job. He was even heavier at that time, bulky, a sloppy nineteen-year-old with a neglected Afro, but she still seemed to like him. He'd done the entire interview with her in Creole, which had won her over. Jessamine, a college senior, was looking for a way to support herself while continuing her studies in nursing. She was lively and confident, but what struck him most about her were the two gold studs she wore on either side of her cheeks. Until she finished her schooling and started working full-time as a pediatric nurse, she was his best hire, his mother's favorite employee. And she was still his best friend.

But where was Jessamine now? he wondered, as he mingled and exchanged pleasantries with his father's friends.

Could she be lost? In the bottleneck traffic that snaked through potholed Route Nationale Numéro 2? Had she been robbed? Kidnapped on the way out of Port-au-Prince?

They had parted ways before his father could see her at the airport. She told him that she had to go see her aunt, after which the cousin who'd picked her up at the airport would see that she got to his father's house in time for the party. He hadn't taken the cousin's phone number. He had been dialing the number at her aunt's house all afternoon, but no one had answered. Maybe her aunt's phone wasn't working. Could the cell phone that Jessamine had brought with her from Miami not be working either?

Max Senior's firm hand was pressing down on his son's shoulder as Max Junior attempted absent-minded small talk with Albert, his father's closest friend. These two men were so close, in fact, that sometimes it seemed as if they were living the same life, following, if not the same career, the same emotional path.

'You've been gone too long,' Albert told Max Junior, his hands shaking, as they always had, even when Max Junior was a boy. The fedora that Oncle Albert – as Max Junior still liked to think of him – always carried with him was meant to shield his shaky hand, but it only brought more attention to it, especially when it fell and he had to bend down and pick it up.

Rumor had it that the shaking was the reason Albert's wife was living near their fifteen-year-old twin son and daughter's boarding school in Massachusetts, while he was running a funeral parlor that had been in their family now for four generations.

'Where's your girl?' Max Senior asked his son.

'My girlfriend?' Albert interrupted, laughing. 'She and my wife don't get along so I didn't bring her.'

Max Junior remained quiet, feeling out of step now with the two men's long-standing comic banter.

Albert's tall and elegant wife, younger by two decades, was indeed in town. She was standing in the back of the living room, by the bookshelves, chatting with a small group of expatriate wives, as his father liked to call them, women who lived in different countries than their husbands did, and when they returned for visits, were never quite at ease or appropriately dressed, wearing leather boots in May, or shorts in December, or any other time of the year. Katya Vincent looked like she had gained only a few pounds since Max Junior had seen her more than ten years ago, but he recalled his father saying of the so-called expatriate wives that they came back each time fatter and reeking of citronella, every mosquito and salad and untreated glass of water suddenly their mortal enemy.

Max Junior remembered being the ring bearer at Katya and Albert Vincent's wedding. His parents had hosted one of the engagement parties. His father had been the best man. It was a time in his life that he sometimes wished he could have back. But as he later came to realize, his mother – and perhaps Katya Vincent too – had never been happy here. His mother, particularly, had always considered her life elsewhere, in the countries that the foreign embassies and cultural alliance organizations represented, and, unlike Katya Vincent, his mother couldn't both escape Ville Rose and hang on to her husband at the same time.

'How is running the town?' Max Junior asked Albert.

'I'm told that some executioners cross themselves before they shoot their victims,' Albert said. He had a gentle, melodious voice, almost soothing to Max Junior's ear. Max Junior had always liked his voice. Unlike his father, who sounded like he was fighting back a stutter, Albert spoke like a singer, a singer of seductive boleros or love songs, which would be great, Max Junior thought, for his new political career. 'I wish I had seen all the voters cross themselves before they cast their ballots for me,' Albert said. 'When something goes right, the national government takes credit. When something goes wrong, I get the blame.'

'That's politics, isn't it?' Max Junior said.

'That's life,' his father added.

'In the end, I see them all, though,' Albert said, 'both victim and executioner.'

'Does that give you the right to insert this type of death talk into every conversation?' asked Max Senior.

'I wanted to talk about wives and girlfriends, but you wouldn't let me,' Albert said, once again laughing his generous, melodious laugh.

'Do you have bodyguards now?' Max Junior asked Albert. 'Security?'

'Why would I?' Albert said. 'If someone wants to kill me,

they'll just shoot the bodyguards first, then me. I'm saving the town money and the criminals bullets.'

Albert then started across the room, heading for his wife. Max Junior watched his father's friend place his arms around a woman who many believed had married him only for his money. She had even taken his children away from him, his father liked to say, locking them up in that boarding school, where they must spend their time mostly hating their country. Indeed, the twins didn't like to return to Ville Rose, choosing winter excursions with their friends and summer camps in France over visiting their father, whose obligation it was always to visit them. One day they would return, Max Junior was certain, when it was time for them to cash in the funeral parlor or take it over.

'Why didn't you send the chauffeur for your girl?' Max Senior now asked his son.

'I don't know about chauffeurs and girlfriends,' Max Junior cracked. He imagined the punch line coming out of Oncle Albert's mouth. 'I've lost many good ones that way. Many good chauffeurs, that is.'

Later in the evening, Max Junior was moved when his father stood at the top of the stairs in front of a room full of his friends and delivered a brief welcome.

'I'm glad my son is back,' his father said while raising his Champagne glass clear above his head. 'I don't know how I have survived here so long without him.'

He had run a school most of his life, but public speaking was not the old man's forte, which made his gesture that much more meaningful to Max Junior. When it was his own turn to speak, he followed his father's example and kept it brief. Standing stiffly at the old man's side, he said, 'It's good to be home, if only for a while.'

'Only awhile?' his father shouted, feigning surprise, as a room full of Champagne glasses clinked once more.

But between all the talk and casual chatter with his father and his guests, all Max Junior could think of was the reason he'd had to leave Ville Rose and Haiti in the first place and whether or not he would ever see Jessamine again.

That night, after everyone had left and his father had gone to bed, Max Junior kept calling Jessamine's Miami cell phone, only to get a busy signal. No matter how late it was, he would have gone to look for her, except he had no idea where her aunt lived in Port-au-Prince. How stupid of him not to have asked her in advance!

He'd been too nervous about this trip to think all the details through. But could his carelessness mean that he would not need Jessamine here as much as he'd thought? In Miami she was the only person to whom he could speak openly about everything. Too damaged herself to be judgmental, she listened to all his confessions with a blank face. She was the only girl he'd told, for example, that he'd fathered a child ten years ago, a child whose name he didn't even know, a child whom he had never met.

As he lay on his back in the same room he'd slept in since he was a boy, Max Junior hit the redial button for Jessamine's cell phone number again and again. His bedroom felt unbearably hot, so he got up and opened the shuttered terrace door that overlooked the peanut-shaped pool and screened gazebo and the maid's quarters for both his father's house and the house next door. Looking up at the sky, he took in the glow of a cluster of stars, something he was never able to see in Miami.

He should be driving all over Port-au-Prince looking for Jessamine, he thought. Isn't that what he should be doing, instead of dialing her number every five minutes while watching the sky? He should be looking for her. Just as he should have been looking for Bernard Dorien a decade before. He should have at least come home for Bernard's funeral. Bernard's parents had probably taken his body to the mountains and buried him there. He felt burdened by the thought of Bernard being suspended somewhere in a hillside grave. To fight so much to live in town, then to return to a mountainside grave? What was the use of sacrificing so much to leave a place, only to end up exactly where you'd started? But wasn't he doing the same thing now, in returning home, looking back when he should be moving forward?

He thought of going for a late-night swim to calm himself, then nixed the idea. Instead, he went back to bed and called Jessamine's number, only to get the same busy signal.

The generator had already been shut down for the night. The ration of electricity allowed for their part of town had expired. So he had no choice but to lie in the dark, in his swimming trunks, his eyes seared open.

When he woke up midmorning the next day and got the first busy signal from Jessamine's phone, he thought of borrowing his father's Jeep and heading out to Port-au-Prince. But then he heard a knock on his bedroom door.

Before he had a chance to collect himself, his father walked in, wearing the gunmetal-gray sweat suit in which he practiced his judo, alone, against a star fruit tree in his garden every morning.

'You have a visitor,' his father said.

'Jessamine?' he asked, grabbing a pair of khakis from the back of a nearby chair and throwing them on.

'Who did you say?' his father asked, moving closer to help him into his pants.

'Is it Jessamine?'

'The one who didn't come last night?'

'Is she down there?'

Max Junior then threw on a red T-shirt that Jessamine had given him long ago, as a gift for hiring her at the Little Haiti sandwich shop. He had promised her that he would wear the shirt when he returned to Haiti since it was half the color of the Haitian flag.

Both the khakis and T-shirt were a bit wrinkled, but

he didn't care. He was about to run out the door when his father grabbed him by an elbow and held him back. Though the old man's salt-and-pepper hair had grown grayer and he had become thicker and slower with each visit to see his son in Miami, and though the old man occasionally complained about his achy shoulders and back, he was still pretty strong. If they ever got into a tussle, Max Junior thought his father could easily throw him.

'Listen to me,' his father said. 'Hold still. Calm. Are you supposed to be in love with this one, what's her name, this Dessalines woman?'

'Jessamine.'

'Anyway, are you in love with her?'

'Papa,' he said, both plea and protest. 'What are you asking me?'

'You liked Flore too, didn't you?' the old man asked.

His father's grip tightened on his biceps. He would have to shove the old man aside to get past him and out the door. He was not of the proper mind-set to think this through in any kind of detail. 'Papa, this is no time,' he said, trying hard not to raise his voice.

'Yes, actually it is a good time,' his father said, 'because Flore is down there right now. And she's with your son.'

'Flore?'

'In the flesh,' the old man said, releasing him. 'En chair et en os, with your son.'

Max didn't remember climbing down the stairs. He simply felt his feet skipping over them two at a time until he was at the bottom. From where he was standing, on the other side of the room, he could first see the back of a woman in an off-the-shoulder mango-colored dress. The woman's hair was short but meticulously curled, as though each strand had been separately attended to. When she finally turned around, he saw that she was wearing lipstick that made her lips look as red as cherries.

It was Flore, but not really Flore. It was Flore, but no longer a skinny teenage girl who wore the same beige maid's uniform that was sometimes stained from food and dirt she picked up in the kitchens and bathrooms of his father's house. It was Flore, but not really Flore, who was now a fierce, older-looking sienna-brown woman. The whole series of incidents – his having had sex with her, her having gotten pregnant – were all in this woman who was standing a few feet from him now.

'Flore?' he asked, more as a request for confirmation than a greeting.

She bobbed her head in his direction but said nothing.

'How have you been?' he asked her, his eyes still taking in all that she had become. 'What are you doing here?'

He didn't mean it to sound like a rebuke. He was genuinely curious, interested in how she had gotten there, back into his father's house, in his father's living room, in the middle of the day.

'Flore has a beauty shop in Port-au-Prince,' his father answered instead. 'I asked her to come see us.'

Max Junior was trying to think of a way to ask about his

son when he heard a child's voice call out from behind the divan, where Flore had walked over to sit.

'Kounye ya? Now?' asked a boy's voice.

'Wi,' said Flore.

Shy, as Flore had been before she'd so drastically changed in face and in body – but also in attitude, it seemed, for Flore's eyes never wavered from his, her face never softened – the child kept his eyes on Max Junior as he pulled a massive grape-colored lollipop in and out of his mouth. The boy was wearing a plain white T-shirt and jeans, and though he was obviously aware that he was the focus of everyone's attention, he took time to survey the room, examining the giant bamboo planters behind the ancient leather couches and the massive abstract paintings on the walls. The boy grimaced at the paintings, large fluorescent blots, which made no sense to Max Junior either. He looked stocky and strong, but Max Junior didn't know many children his age, so he wasn't sure. Neither he nor his father was a lean man. They were men of average height, paunchy and round, like this boy might one day be, when he grew up. As a matter of fact, the boy looked exactly like them, like he might fall perfectly in line with all the generations of men in his family.

'And what do you do with him for school in Port-au-Prince?' Max Senior asked from behind the banister, where he was now sitting. 'Is he getting some good schooling? You know very well, Flore, that we have a school here, a good one.'

Shifting a small, woven straw purse from one shoulder to

the other, Flore gazed around the room as though searching for an anchor for herself. 'He's well, as you can see,' she said.

Max Junior was now standing right in front of his son and his son was looking up at him and he was looking down at his son. He kneeled so that his face was at the level of his son's and said, 'Alo.'

'Alo,' the boy echoed, with the lollipop still lodged in one of his cheeks.

For a moment Max Junior worried that the child might leap at him and tackle him to the ground as his own father watched from behind the banister. 'My name is Maxime Ardin, Jr.,' he said.

Max Junior thought the boy a handsome child, a stoop-shouldered little boy with an open face and generous smile. Max Junior himself had been a boy like that. He waited for the child to say his name. Thought for a moment that he might not. The boy looked over at his mother for some clue as to what he should do. She tilted her head and seemed as eager to hear what would come out of the boy's mouth as Max Junior was.

'My name is Pamaxime Voltaire,' the child said.

Because Max Junior had not legally recognized the boy, the child had been given Flore's family name, Voltaire. But with 'Pa,' a Creole prefix meaning both 'his' and 'not his,' the child's first name could either mean 'Maxime's' or 'Not Maxime's.' Only the mother could know for sure.

'Pamaxime,' Max repeated, copying the child's hesitant voice.

It surprised him that Flore had named the child this way.

'If he were a girl, we could at least call him Pam,' Max Senior said, drawing a stern, hateful look from Flore.

Looking back at Flore, who gave Pamaxime a small nod of approval for the perfect enunciation of his name, the child, still with the lollipop in his mouth and with a coy voice that sounded a bit rehearsed, asked, 'Ou se papa m? Are you my papa?'

'Wi,' Max Junior said. He was amazed how quickly the word came out of his mouth. Though he had not offered Pamaxime the family name, now looking at his child's face, he was even more certain that this boy was his, in spite of or because of the negation or affirmation of his own name.

Kneeling there next to his son, Max Junior remembered a story Jessamine had told him when he'd confessed to her that he was thinking of coming home for a visit. Jessamine's parents had met in Miami while working at a hotel where her mother and father were both part of the cleaning staff. Soon after they got married, her father decided to return to Haiti to live. Her mother stayed behind in Miami, promising to join him in a few weeks. During that time, her mother discovered that she was pregnant with Jessamine and, no longer wanting to move to Haiti, filed for divorce. Her father didn't know about Jessamine until she was in her first year of high school and he, sick and dying from something or other, returned to Miami for treatment. In the meantime, Jessamine had been told by her mother that her father had abandoned her. Jessamine hadn't seen her father live and wasn't sure she wanted to see him die. She went with her mother to visit him in the hospital anyway. Right before they got there, he took his last breath. They were allowed to stay in the room with the body for only a few minutes before her father was wheeled out under a white sheet and taken down to the morgue.

Ever since Jessamine had told him about her own father, Max Junior had replayed that scene in the hospital over and over in his mind, casting his son in Jessamine's role and himself as the dead father on the gurney being rolled out. The worst possible case of unrequited love, Jessamine had told him, was feeling abandoned by a parent.

Both he and his son were in a mild trance now, their eyes locked on each other's, which he became aware of only when Flore snapped her fingers and whistled, motioning for the boy to walk to her. The Flore he knew before would have never made such crude gestures.

Pamaxime was still standing in front of him. He wanted to reach over and take his son in his arms now, but he was afraid of overwhelming the child. In her continued attempt to capture the boy's attention, Flore clapped and clapped again, yet the child did not move. Looking back and forth between him and Flore, he seemed torn. The boy looked at Max Senior, his grandfather, who motioned with his index finger for Pamaxime to go to Flore.

'Why such a hurry?' Max Senior then said. 'Let the child

stay here a day or two. Let's see more of him. He can play, have a swim with us in the pool.'

The child turned to Max Senior, who was now standing with both his hands in the air as though pleading to the heavens for a special favor.

'He will not stay here,' Flore said, as though she were speaking from behind a grille locked inside her mouth.

And with those words, Flore rushed forward and grabbed Pamaxime's hand, but he did not move. Max Junior tried to reach for the boy's other hand, the one farther from Flore, not to stroke or kiss, but just to touch him to say a tactile good-bye. But before he could, the boy was led away by his mother. Reaching down, Flore motioned for the boy to hand her the remainder of the lollipop, then dropped it in her purse.

Max Junior was still kneeling there as his son walked off. The child did not turn around. He remained on his knees, hoping that the boy might run back, to hug or kiss him, to tell him his first good-bye after his first hello. But what had he done to deserve it?

He heard some voices coming from the next room, by the front door. It was Flore talking to an older woman, who, though she'd been working for his father now many years, he could only think of as the new maid. It seemed that Pamaxime had something he wanted to give him, and Flore was asking the new maid to take it, so the child wouldn't have to come back. Max Junior thought of running out to collect it, but stopped himself. Flore had every right to make all the decisions.

He heard the front door slam shut.

'From the child.' The new maid handed him a folded piece of white paper.

He could feel his father watching him. Back when he had his music show at Radio Zòrèy, he had gotten notes dropped off for him at the station and at home all the time. Many of the girls had handed the perfume-scented missives to Flore at his front door.

He opened the sheet of paper his son had brought for him. On it was the word 'papa' in small slanted letters along with a sketch of a man with a blank 0 for a face. He yearned for an explanation that he knew he might never get. He folded the paper and placed it in his pants pocket, then he rose from the floor and rushed out the door. His father followed, as though both he and the old man had come to the same conclusion at once.

A tiled driveway parted the lush tropical garden that led from Max Senior's porch to his front gate.

'Tann,' Max Junior called out after Flore. 'Wait.'

Flore spun around and the child did the same, mimicking his mother. Max Junior caught up with them near where his father's car was parked, by the low iron gates.

'Let me take you wherever you're going,' Max Junior said.

He imagined they were going back to Flore's mother's house in Cité Pendue. While stroking his son's closely cropped hair, he added, 'Mwen la kounye a. I'm here now.'

The boy squirmed and craned his neck so he could see both his father and his mother at the same time. Max Junior felt as though he were in a public square as his father watched from a wooden bench on his front porch. But none of it mattered. He was no longer a nineteen-year-old boy. He was an adult now, a man who shared a child with this woman.

His father walked over from the bench and placed himself at the boy's side.

'Can I borrow your car to take them home?' Max Junior asked his father.

Flore raised her eyebrows in surprise.

'Would you know the way?' Max Senior asked his son.

Max Junior nodded.

Max Senior walked back into the house and returned with the keys to his tèt bèf, everyone's cow-horn nickname for this kind of Toyota Jeep. He handed the keys to his son, then walked to the front gates, sliding them open, for the car to pass through. He walked back to his front porch and, before he went into his house, called out, 'Bye!' to his grandson. But the boy didn't even glance at him; he was too busy paying attention to his own father to hear.

First Max Junior helped the boy into the car. This gave him another opportunity to touch his son as he held the child's hands, guiding him to settle in the backseat. He tried to pull the seat belt across the boy's chest. The straps rose to the child's neck, so he decided to forgo it. He shut the door, opened the passenger side for Flore, then finally climbed into the driver's seat. The hem of Flore's dress rose high above her knees as she settled into her seat and quickly she pulled it down. She could have sat in the back with the child, making him feel like their chauffeur, but she didn't.

He had never been deep inside Cité Pendue. He had only driven with his parents, on their way farther south, by the main road that circled it, the road by the sea. Still he felt as though he had already been there. He'd been there in the way his friend Bernard Dorien had described his parents' restaurant, which was, according to Bernard, practically attached to the Rue des Saints warehouse, once occupied by the men of Baz Benin. He'd been there through the music that the Baz Benin men had produced and recorded and brought to him on CDs and even cassettes, to play on his radio program, their praise of and laments about precarious life and certain death in the geto.

'What's a good way?' he asked Flore as he turned the Jeep toward a line of calabash trees in front of his father's gate. Ten years before, it would have been best to use the road by the sea, but he wasn't sure anymore and wanted to confirm this with her. And she agreed with a reluctant nod.

Even after ten years, the road along the sea was still tarred and mostly paved. There were more cars now, and the traffic crept along the two wide lanes going in opposite directions.

Several young men and women tapped on the car window, offering to sell him fried foods and meats, plantain chips, and bottled water. Others followed, hawking cell phone chargers and batteries.

In the cars and camions in front and on the other side of him, he saw that many of his fellow drivers and their passengers passed the time by talking on cell phones, something which, a decade before, when he'd left the country, you wouldn't have seen. On the opposite side, a funeral procession was stuck in the gridlock with a hearse leading a small caravan of cars that motto taxis snaked through.

When the traffic did move along, it reminded him how pretty Ville Rose still was. On one side of them were the same moss-blanketed marshes he remembered from years ago and in the distance some funnel-shaped mountains.

Soon, though, they passed a new line of low-grade brothels, where women sold sex in individual bungalows. A loud bell sounded in Flore's purse and she pulled out a cell phone, then switched off the ringer. She turned around and handed the phone to the boy, and occasionally when Max Junior looked in the rearview mirror, he would see the boy tapping the keys hard and fast while playing some kind of game. He realized that he had forgotten his own cell phone in his room at his father's house.

Glancing now and then at Flore's profile, which she kept nearly frozen, almost like a statue, he found it difficult to remember most of what they'd once talked about. It was never consequential, nothing ever too deep. Aside from the usual things about what he wanted her to cook on a particular day, he would try to make her laugh with him at the lovestricken girls who wrote him letters, for example, but she never did. He would make fun of some friend of his father's who had come to dinner with his wife and met his mistress there – a dinner she had served them. She would never join in his teasing and criticism.

Back then, she'd seemed interested in magazines, especially the beauty magazines left behind by his father's female friends. He would sometimes catch her staring at the women in those pages, her mouth open, her eyes widened in awe. He would try to bring home more of those magazines from the radio station, as many as he could, and he would leave them lying around the house for her to pick up and look through when he was out. She often straightened her own hair with a box of relaxer she'd buy from a vendor of hair extensions at the open market, but they never discussed any of that. They never even discussed how she had come to his father's house when she was barely sixteen, why she had been made to leave school to replace an aunt who'd worked there for years until the aunt was too old to work.

The child was still lost in the cell phone game, pounding the keys even harder now, as though there were something dire at stake.

'Why did you name him that?' he asked her quietly.

'What?' she snapped, without turning her face.

'Why did you give him such a name?' He did not even want to say it so as not to bring the child's attention to their conversation.

'Because I wanted to,' Flore said.

But what he meant to ask her was which way she'd intended the name. Not his? Or his? But he couldn't think of a way to ask without the child understanding exactly what they were talking about. He looked back in the rearview mirror, and the boy now had the phone closed on his lap and his thumb wedged in his mouth.

'Aren't you too old for that?' he asked the boy.

The child pulled his finger out of his mouth and placed his hands on the seat, under his thighs.

'I've tried so many things,' Flore said, more to the boy than to him. 'Even rubbed a hot pepper on it.'

'A hot pepper?' Max Junior grimaced. 'Terrible.'

When it grew quiet in the car again, Max Junior turned on the radio. A newscaster was droning on about demonstrations against high food prices in Port-au-Prince. Could Jessamine have been caught up in that? Could that have kept her from making it to Ville Rose either last night or this morning? It already felt like weeks since he had seen her, although it had been only twenty-four hours.

'Are there any children's programs on Radio Zòrèy the way there used to be?' he asked, trying to think of some other way to entertain the child.

Flore shrugged. She either didn't know or didn't care.

When Max Junior looked back in the rearview mirror, he

saw the boy was now asleep, lying across the backseat with both his legs fully bent. He was indeed a beautiful boy, Max Junior thought, not just handsome, but beautiful. It was a kind of beauty that he thought everyone could admire. No one could look at this child sleeping, his eyes tightly closed, his chest rising up and falling down, his face so relaxed that he looked defenseless, no one could look at that child, he thought, and not find him free of blame and shame.

It had taken nearly ninety minutes to drive eight miles, but they were finally entering Cité Pendue. He could tell by the way the sea on the side of the road had turned from green-blue to brown to ashen black. The streets narrowed, rising in a line of sloped hills packed with cement and cinderblock homes, tin shacks, and open markets filled with exhausted-looking women and wilted food.

'The house isn't too far in.' Flore was guiding him. 'My mother wanted something not far from the street.'

He turned a narrow corner that seemed like it was never made for a car to pass through, then down a crisscrossed trail, where he finally found the house.

It was different from what he'd expected, prettier. Box-shaped with pink grille metalwork covering the front. He tried to park the car as close to the front as possible and leave room in the narrow alley for people to walk by.

The boy was still asleep in the back. Max Junior picked him up, cradling him in his arms. This is what it must have felt like to hold him as a baby, he thought. A very heavy baby. The child was breathing deeply, and when he pushed the boy's body into his chest, the child wriggled, twisting himself back in place.

'Where should I put him?' Max Junior asked once Flore opened the front door.

Inside, the house smelled overpoweringly of vanilla essence, the liquid type you might add to lemonade and cakes. The living room was sparse, with four plastic-covered chairs facing one another across a narrow table pushed against a back corner. A lightbulb dangled on a cable from the ceiling and on the walls were beauty-queen calendars, advertising beer and skin-bleaching soaps and creams.

A bamboo curtain hid a bedroom with a large bed that took up most of the room, along with two large stuffed-looking suitcases. As he placed Pamaxime on the bed, Flore turned on a standing fan and aimed it in the sleeping child's direction. Flore seemed surprised that the fan came on, that there was any electricity at all.

'Where's your mother?' he asked when they stepped back into the front room.

'In the market,' she said.

His nose full of the vanilla essence – his eyes nearly watering from it – he was filled with regret, but did not know how to tell her. In the end, in spite of these surroundings, she seemed to have somehow triumphed. She had now proved, by letting him meet his son, for one thing, that she was no longer afraid of him. And what had he done? He'd brought into the world a child whom he had ignored. He'd left his home and his country for years. And he'd kept secrets.

'I'm sorry, Flore. I'm sorry for what was done,' he said, pacing now, across a cement floor that was as uneven as the ceiling.

'What was done? You mean for what you did.' She seemed to have been waiting for him to bring up the subject – or dreading that he would. Her arms began shaking as she tried to dust one of the plastic-covered chairs with her bare palms. She rubbed her hands together, then balled both her fists as though she were getting ready to punch him. He could tell that her anger had been simmering not just today, but for the last ten years, and now that she was in her own neighborhood, in her mother's house, she could release it.

'I went there today,' she said, 'because your father found us in Port-au-Prince and asked me to come. But now? No, no, I don't want to see you again.'

Looking around the room, which was a fifth the size of his room at his father's house, he thought that it could use a window. A window might take away some of this awful vanilla-essence fragrance. It might let in more light. It might allow the boy to see the sky when he woke up from his sleep. A window might make the entire house feel bigger, make them feel freer. A window and some plants, like some of the plants in his father's garden, were what this little house needed, he thought. But the spot in the wall where the window might be was needed for the neighbor's wall, and a window might make them less safe here. A window might make it easier for someone else to come in and hurt them.

'What about the boy?' he asked, because everything was now centered on the boy. The boy was everything. 'He drew me,' he said. How could the boy have known what he would look like? What would he have drawn if he'd been asked to sketch the boy? 'He drew me without a face. Just a circle, a blank circle.'

'Did you want your face to look like an ass?' she asked, a triumphant smirk flashing across her mouth. She tried to suppress it, but it remained there, like her own personal victory.

A decade ago, he'd tried to convince himself that he might love her, that he might want to make a life with her. He tried to make himself believe that this would be best. But this was one of many false dreams he held close to his heart, like the one of finally making love to a woman who could fully satisfy him, whom he would long for and miss every morning when he woke up.

'I'd like to contribute,' he said, now raising his head to examine the slab-sided pink ceiling above their heads. 'I'd like to contribute to a good school in Port-au-Prince. A school like Papa's school.'

'Your father gave me some money,' she said. 'Your mother sent me some too. You must know that.'

Actually he did not know that. He found it easier to believe that his mother would wire her money from Miami, but not that his father would hand Flore some. Or that this was something his parents would do together.

Flore walked to the door, grabbed the wobbly metal handle to open it, then motioned with an abrupt movement of her head for him to leave. He reached into his pocket for his wallet nevertheless, but he'd left his father's house in too much haste and, along with his cell phone, had also left behind his wallet. He made a gesture toward her, but, pushing his empty hands away, she said, 'Ale tanpri. Please go.'

She followed him out. He muttered hello to some of her neighbors, who were sitting out on their cement porches as he climbed into the Jeep.

'Where can I find Rue des Saints?' he asked once he'd slouched down behind the wheel.

Flore looked up at the closest neighbors, two women, one old, one young, and a teenage boy who seemed to be the older woman's grandson. A curious look passed between her and her neighbors. Had Flore told them, told everyone, about what he'd done?

'Rue des Saints is no longer Rue des Saints, I know,' he said to the young man. 'I just want to find out how to get there.'

He'd heard about it in Miami. The morning he'd left Ville Rose, Bernard Dorien had been arrested. The next day he was found dead. Then someone had set fire to Baz Benin, a fire that not only had destroyed Baz Benin but, as it spread, had razed Bè, Bernard's parents' restaurant. He didn't know where Bernard's parents were spending the rest of their lives. (Had they returned to the mountains? Did they start another restaurant elsewhere?) In the Haitian newpapers he'd read in Miami, only Tiye and his lieutenant, Piye, had been listed as having died in the fire.

This cascading news had shattered him, but there was nothing he could do from Miami. Or was there? Even if he'd returned to Haiti, Bernard would still be gone and his parents' business too. There was nothing he could have done.

'Can I still get to Rue des Saints?' Max Junior asked.

The young man used the life lines in Max Junior's palms as coordinates on an imaginary map. Max Junior followed his directions, driving nearly a half hour between tin shacks on dirt roads before he reached Rue des Saints.

The street that was once Rue des Saints was now mostly a row of wooden shacks next to a reeking landfill smoldering on the edge of an oil-streaked storm drain. Max Junior stopped the car. On both sides of him were mountains of trash, tires, and thousands of tiny plastic juice bottles and foam food containers. A few people stopped to stare at him before continuing on their way: two old women returning from the market, a group of sweaty boys taking turns clutching a ball on their way home from a soccer game. If not for those people, it would have been impossible for him to imagine that this had ever been the kind of place where people lived, where his friend Bernard had lived.

Sitting in the car, he thought of the last time he'd seen Bernard. Bernard had been typing a news script at the radio station and had taken a moment to look up and invite him for a meal at his parents' restaurant. Max had been too embarrassed to tell Bernard he was afraid to go there.

The windows were closed now. Still the fetid smell of decomposing trash penetrated the car and was nearly choking him. Max Junior started the engine and kept driving until he found the sea once again. He followed the sea out of Cité Pendue until it turned a robin's egg blue, the Ville Rose color he had longed for most when he was in Miami.

He rolled down the windows, and with a hot gust of air blasting his face, spent all afternoon going home. He allowed himself to linger in the bottleneck traffic, then he realized that it had been some time now since he'd thought about Jessamine. He looked in the tight wedge between the driver's seat cushion and backrest and found the white envelope with the five-hundred-gourde note his father always kept there for emergencies. He stopped at a street corner for fried plantains, goat, and pork, which he ate from a dented metal plate in front of the vendor's pot of sizzling oil, then washed it all down with a bottle of imported fluorescent juice. Leaving the food vendor's, he drove slowly, purposely taking the wrong turns, stopping to sit on the side of smaller streets and out-of-the-way trails before returning to the busy main thoroughfare by the sea.

It was nearly dark when he pulled up in front of his father's house and saw Jessamine sitting with his father on the brightly lit front porch. She was wearing dark leggings and a plain white tunic top, yet still looked elegant, as though she were heading out to a ball. Both Jessamine and his father saw the Jeep through the open gate. He lowered his head, pretending he had some task to complete in the car before he could come out. A radio program was blaring from one of the neighboring houses and he could have sworn he heard Flore's voice on it. But that couldn't be right. He had left Flore in Cité Pendue not that long ago.

A bouncy commercial jingle cut off the Flore-like voice. It was followed by a loud pitchman touting health shakes, cigarettes, and beer in the same breathless voice. He stopped paying attention. He was contemplating instead the fact that Jessamine didn't call out his name or run to him.

Watching her and his father sip something or other, he imagined his father learning that Jessamine was a nurse and asking her for medical advice about his old judo injuries. He imagined them talking about his father's paintings, his garden and flowers. But he could imagine Jessamine having also told his father how she was not really his girlfriend and how she had agreed to come with him just so his father would think he had a girlfriend, and how they had even debated whether he should buy her a ring and call her his fiancée. Maybe she was telling his father how she had agreed to come with him, as a good and loyal friend, only so that he would come and meet his son.

His father got up and waved. Though he didn't move from behind the wheel, he waved back, indicating he was coming. It was obvious that Jessamine had already conquered his father, most likely with compliments about the town, the house. Or maybe his father was overly impressed that though she was born in Miami, she could still speak Creole, even with an accent. Jessamine was glad, he knew, to see the place that had, in part, made him.

The commercial jingles continued on his father's neighbor's radio. A scripted dialogue between two popular comedians about two competing cell phone companies was playing now. Max Junior wondered whether if he were still living in this town – not in his father's house, but in a house of his own – he might feel obligated to drive by every afternoon to see if his father was all right. Might he also sit outside, in a car, feeling grateful that he'd escaped this house and its rueful memories? He pretended that he was actually inside this moment that would never be, and the second both Jessamine and his father turned their faces away from him and toward each other, he started the car and drove away. He sped forward, heading down Pied Rose Avenue toward the beach.

One way he had delayed accepting Bernard's invitation to his parents' restaurant in Cité Pendue was to invite Bernard to the beach. They would go to the lagoons, then dive in and out of the reefs. Every once in a while they'd spot a large flying fish or a sea turtle, which were as mythic as ghost crabs because they were so rare. At night, they would walk up to the Anthère lighthouse, climb the winding staircase, and lie on the gallery floor in the dark to better see the stars.

He had left Ville Rose the day before Bernard was killed.

Flore had told his father that she was pregnant with his child, and his father had sent him to his mother in Miami. He was nineteen, banished from his home for creating a life just at the moment when his friend lay dying. The irony of this was still weighing on him.

When Max Junior arrived at the beach that evening, he saw a crowd gathered around a large-legged woman who was speaking to everyone with her hands. She was wearing a dark scarf around her head, which nearly swallowed her face.

Next to her, a fisherman, a man the people were calling Nozias, leaned in. He was interpreting the movements of the woman's hands. She held both hands toward the crowd, one palm facing the dimming light of the early-evening sky and the other facing the sand, then she reversed them, the sand palm now fixed at the sky and the sky palm aimed at the sand.

'Mouri,' the man next to her said. 'Dead. She thinks he's dead.'

Dead. This single word seemed the proper conclusion to Max Junior's day.

He spent the rest of the evening under a dense grove of palms that had grown in a curve, their intricate roots spilling over the sand. He bought a bottle of Prestige beer, which he drank before dozing off at the foot of the crescent palms.

When he woke up, a bonfire had been started and the

dead fisherman's wife was sitting in its glow, in a low sisal chair, receiving well-wishers. Too large for her long white skirt to fully cover, her heavier leg looked like a piece of driftwood waiting to be placed in the fire.

Watching the dead fisherman's wife reminded him of a Grimm's fairy tale his father had told him when he was a boy. The way he remembered it, one day a fisherman pulled a talking flounder out of the sea. Claiming to be an enchanted prince, the flounder begged to be returned to the sea and the fisherman released him. When the fisherman went home, he told his wife what had happened, and she scolded him for asking nothing of the enchanted flounder in return for his release. The fisherman's wife convinced her husband to return to the sea, find the flounder, and ask him for a cottage to replace the shack in which they were living. The flounder granted the wife's wish and soon they had a cottage. This was not enough for the wife, who made her husband return several times to ask the flounder for a castle, then to make her an emperor, then a pope, then a god.

The part that Max Junior remembered best – because it was the part of the story that his father seemed to disapprove of the most – was of the wife wanting the power to make the sun rise.

What is wrong with wanting that? Max Junior had always thought. Who wouldn't want the power to make the sun rise at will?

He now found himself in the somewhat familiar predicament of being a so-called rich boy who was out of money. His head ached. He was hungry again. Where was his enchanted flounder? he wondered.

He thought of returning home, but how would he explain his having left so abruptly? His father would be angry with him. Jessamine would probably be angry too. Still, they had not come looking for him. They both should have known where he might be.

Max Junior got up and walked through the small crowd of people still gathered on the beach. Then, just as the fisherman's wake was drawing to a close, a father began crying out his daughter's name, and people joined in looking for her. The father of the missing daughter was the fisherman Nozias, the one who had been interpreting the fisherman's wife's movements for the others.

Max drifted in and out of different sections of the crowd, and he did as they did, hollering, 'Claire!' the missing girl's name.

The name was as buoyant as it sounded. It was the kind of name that you said with love, that you whispered in your woman's ears the night before your child was born. It was the kind of name you could easily carry in your dreams, in your mouth, the kind of name that made you clasp your hands against your chest when you heard it being shouted out of so many mouths. It was the kind of name you might find in poems or love letters, or songs. It was a love name and not a revenge name. It was the kind of name that you could call out with hope. It was the kind of name that had the power to make the sun rise.

But soon everyone stopped calling the girl's name and began to drift away. And when he looked up at the hills, he saw that even the people who had been flashing lights from the lighthouse gallery were also gone.

When it came to the town's mores, he was now at a disadvantage, after being away so long. He was no longer aware of who was sleeping with whom, or who was allowed to sleep with whom, without causing a scandal. And yet just then he thought he saw his parents' old friend Gaëlle Lavaud go into one of the fishermen's shacks. He had some vague recollection of his father telling him that they were to have dinner at her house one night before he returned to Miami. Was that really her? Was she now his father's lover or the fisherman Nozias's lover? Or both?

In any case, it seemed that Gaëlle Lavaud and the fisherman Nozias would be sleeping apart. For soon after they went in together, the fisherman left the shack and lay down on the sand between two boulders, confident, it seemed, that his daughter would return. Just as his father might also be certain that he too would soon be home.

Part Two

Starfish

LOUISE GEORGE, HOSTESS OF the radio program *Di Mwen*, had been coughing up blood during her periods ever since she began menstruating at age thirteen. Over the years she had seen many specialists and had many tests, but no doctor could satisfactorily explain how blood from her uterus also showed up in her lungs, then in her mouth. What's worse, no one could tell her why, at fifty-five, she had still not gone through menopause, making it seem as though this could possibly go on forever. And since in Ville Rose all things unexplained were attributed to the spirit world, Louise tried to keep as much to herself as possible when she wasn't taping her radio program.

This was not hard to do because the few people who had seen her bloodstained teeth or handkerchiefs had worried that she might be pwatrinè, or have tuberculosis, and so had stayed away. That is all except Max Ardin, Sr., who not only occasionally slept with her, but would now and then invite her to read to the students at his school.

Max Senior had known Louise long enough to be aware that her condition was rare, but that a certain type of lung surgery or hormone therapy might treat it, though the hormones were extremely expensive and were not yet available in Haiti and the surgery potentially fatal. So Louise got used to tasting her own blood, agonizing about it only on those three or four days a month when she had to completely withdraw from everything and everyone.

During those days when she was home alone, Louise wrote. She wrote about the people in Ville Rose, tidbits she picked up from the gossip mill, or teledyòl, or what she'd gathered over the years from the interviews on her radio show. Her book had begun as an extension of the show, but had grown into a type of choral piece. She called it to herself a collage à clef.

A few nights after she'd gone to read to one of his younger classes, Max Senior called to ask her if she would do him the extra favor of teaching one of the school's adult literacy classes, after he came up with the idea of helping some of the students by teaching their illiterate parents to read. Most of the children who could afford the high tuition at École Ardin had professional parents – public functionaries, business owners – or sponsoring relatives abroad. But there were a few bright students whose parents were indigent, or nearly so. Max Senior had given them scholarships to make their way.

Louise was still dreading her first moments with these scholarship parents when the time came. Unlike the children, the parents wouldn't simply look up at her with glee as she read them some of her favorite stories and poems. But teaching these adults was an opportunity for her not only to use the training she'd gotten as a young woman at the Faculté d'Education in Port-au-Prince, but also to gather potential subjects for her radio show.

The show had begun six months before one of Radio Zòrèy's biggest sponsors, Laurent Lavaud, had been shot right outside the station gates. She didn't know him very well, but she had been one of the last people to see him alive. He'd rushed into the control room to drop off an envelope for the station manager, and she had seen him through the glass during a commercial break.

The next day, a young newswriter at her station had been arrested for Laurent Lavaud's murder, then, soon after, had been murdered himself. She had closely followed the investigation (or lack of it). It was like all police investigations in Haiti. At first it was all everyone was talking about, then it went cold, and then for years, whenever it came up, everyone from the chief of police to journalism students would say 'L'enquête se poursuit. The investigation continues.' Even though it had not.

After those deaths and others, she had considered changing the format of the show from one that allowed people to air personal grievances to one that pursued justice. She'd thought of renaming the show *Seriatim,* the Latin word for 'series.' She'd also considered *Verbatim* or *Word for Word,* or the legal term that combined both, but she didn't want the station's core audience of plain and regular people to be put off. Hearing Latin once or twice a week at Mass was probably all they could bear. So now she found herself doing only confessional, but sometimes accusatory, interviews. The show's very large audience favored gossipy subjects over true crime, unless there were elements of gossip in the crime. She liked to start the hour by welcoming her guests with the words 'Di mwen.' 'Tell me,' she would say. 'We are ready to hear your story.'

Before the charity parents showed up at Max Senior's school that night, Louise suddenly got cold feet. Over the years, her gaunt body had grown even tinier, making her look, in the different shades of purple dresses she always wore, more like a nun than a popular radio personality. She was such a mystery to most people in town that once, while attending Mass in the town cathedral, she heard a man who was sitting behind her say that it was rumored ke li manje chat, that she ate cats, which implied that she was also an alcoholic, a lonely lush who somehow kept herself under control only to tape her show.

The first parent who arrived for the literacy class was Nozias Faustin, a bald young fisherman. He was dressed in a church-worthy secondhand brown suit with an open-necked white shirt. He was father to Claire Limyè Lanmè Faustin, an attentive little girl from one of the primary-school classes at École Ardin. Claire Limyè Lanmè Faustin's hair was always braided in what seemed to be a hundred yarnlike plaits, each individually fastened with a different colored bow-shaped plastic barrette. Aside from the barrettes, which thankfully had not been in vogue when Louise was a girl, Claire was the one child in the classes she read to who reminded her much of herself when she was young. The girl was so quiet that Louise worried that there might be some other frightful things about Claire that would link them. Had she, also like Louise, been born with absolutely nothing, from people who had absolutely nothing? Was she the surviving twin who had lost a sibling at her birth? Had she been born with a sixth finger on each hand, which had been forced to atrophy by having strings tied tightly around them? Did she have a spider-shaped birthmark on her belly?

The other parent, Odile Désir, was a strapping, scowling woman who, when she showed up, was still wearing her ocher uniform and apron from her job as a server in a restaurant in town. Louise had seen that scowl before and not just on Odile's face. She saw it whenever she was around certain adults. Was it a scowl of fear or pity? Why did it matter in the end? Why should she even care? But this type of self-questioning made her realize even more that she did care. She cared because, just like the people she interviewed every week, she was floating through her life, looking for some notion of who she was, and in those scowls and rumors she often caught a glimpse, even if a distorted one, of what that might be. But that evening at the literacy class for three, it was very clear what she was to Odile Désir: her sworn enemy.

Odile's son, Henri, was by far the worst-behaved student in any class that she had ever read to at Max Senior's school. Even the shy and quiet Claire was not spared Henri's taunts and hair pulling. A restless, rambunctious boy, he had, early in the school year, lost two front milk teeth, which still showed no signs of being replaced by adult ones, a gap he often used to spit at the other children.

'Why me?' Louise had asked Max Senior when he'd first suggested she teach the evening class. 'Surely one of your full-time teachers can do this.'

'Don't you want the satisfaction of being a miracle worker, of making the blind see?' he'd asked, smiling, his face softening in a way that even after all these years still enchanted her.

Ever since they had met at the Faculté – where she was a scholarship student – Louise recalled that Max Senior was always researching educational methods that demanded a lot of those around him. Sometimes she was thrilled by those experiments, like his asking her to tell or read her favorite stories to the children. And other times they annoyed her, like the evening literacy class, which she now wished she'd declined. Sometimes, with all his pedagogical lecturing, framed by his sweet-faced smile, she even wanted to hit Max Ardin. Not hard and not often, just one quick slap. But there were also many times when she found herself feeling grateful to him, because even as he was orchestrating his pedagogical schemes, building his career, getting married and divorced, he never forgot her.

The two parents had only nodded at each other when they arrived that evening. Both looked equally exhausted after long days at physically taxing jobs.

'Why do you want to learn to read?' Louise asked each one in turn.

Henri's mother, Odile, shrugged. 'I don't want people to take me for an imbecile,' she replied, her face a tight mask.

'For Claire,' Claire's father, Nozias, said simply, 'so I can help her with her lessons.'

'Those are both very good reasons,' Louise said, leaning back into the same rocking chair she had demanded that Max Senior provide for her to read to the children, in part to connect her reading to them with the porch-style storytelling sessions of their parents' childhoods.

'I don't want either of you to feel ashamed,' she added. 'You didn't have the opportunities that your children now have.'

Louise had prepared that little speech beforehand, before she'd even known who'd be there. She had also prepared to tell these parents about ancient civilizations whose indigenous populations never knew how to read or write but used hieroglyphs with which it was easy to recognize water as wavy lines, and a man or a bird as a drawing of such. And she reminded them both of the well-known saying 'Analfabèt pa bèt,' or 'Illiterates are not stupid.' But then she got tired of the whole thing and of herself and told them to go home.

On their way out, the two parents stopped by Max Senior's office together to complain, each adding that they had, at

Max Senior's request, gone through a great deal of trouble to get there and that Madame Louise had not properly addressed them.

'Tant pis,' Louise told Max Senior when he recounted their complaints to her in bed later that night. 'Too bad.'

Louise and Max Senior had been sleeping together on and off since the Faculté. They had stopped while he was married and had picked up again after his divorce. Louise was not in love with him; she did not think herself capable of being in love with anyone. Being alone was simpler, the intermingling of lives too confusing and too messy, a fact confirmed for her on her radio show each week.

That night in bed, at her house across from Sainte Rose de Lima Cathedral, Max Senior held one of Louise's hands under the sheets. She dangled the other over the side of the bed and, after a sudden rush of blood to her finger-tips, felt them go numb. Lying there, she wished that she'd agreed, as he had suggested to her one night, to paint her bedroom ceiling in a glow-in-the-dark shade of fluorescent green. Max Senior had once confided to her how when he was a boy he had been deathly afraid of nights without lights, starless and moonless nights without any electricity, nights that he'd called 'Ki moun sa a?' nights, or 'Who are you?' nights, because it was hard to recognize anyone. It was so dark that when you opened your eyes, you saw the same inky gloom as when your eyes were closed, he said. At that time, she'd laughed and said no, she didn't want her bedroom to look like the walls of a kindergarten classroom. But now she thought she might reconsider the glow-in-the-dark paint. If she had a bit of luminescence to stare up at on nights like this, might it be easier to pretend that she was somewhere outside, with blades of grass tickling her cheeks?

'Je voudrais . . .' His words interrupted her thoughts. 'I would like to talk to you about something,' he was saying.

He released her fingers to run his hand across her abdomen, tracing, in the dark, the baby spider birthmark that grew into a full-blown black widow when her stomach swelled during those days she was menstruating.

'What is it?' she asked.

'The school,' he said, moving his face closer to hers in the dark. She wanted to turn away, but instead she pressed her eyelids together so tightly that they made another kind of sky, a sky full of fireflies and tiny torches.

'You slapped one of my students the other day when you came to read,' he said. 'One of the children of the parents who came to the class tonight.'

It was just like him to set her up by bringing those parents there and then try to make a lesson out of the whole thing. He had been that way since the Faculté, always eager to teach someone a lesson in a totally roundabout way.

'The children at our school are never hit on our premises' was often the theme of their school-related pillow talk. That and his insistence that she was a great teacher in a country with so few and that she should have been teaching for decades, and even now could still be teaching. And that she was wasting her time on that show. It was useless for her to keep telling him that she thought she was 'teaching' on her show.

His was one of a few schools in the region with a no-hitting philosophy, which some of the parents welcomed and others detested. Most other schools carried out some type of corporal punishment, from ruler taps on the hand to cowhide straps on the legs and flat-board taps on the bottom. But Max Senior felt that corporal punishment was archaic, even barbaric, and he kept close watch on everyone, especially any teachers accused of abusive practices, to make sure they didn't take place at his school.

'Henri's mother wants to meet with you and me tomorrow afternoon after school.' His voice was tight, distant. And without saying anything more, he turned his back to her so that they were now facing opposite sides of her room.

'Must I go?' she asked, knowing, in spite of having one of the most listened-to voices in town, that she now sounded like a child who was being sent to the headmaster's office. 'I'm not even a teacher at the school.'

'This must be resolved,' he said. 'And I hope you will grant me and this boy and his mother that courtesy.'

It wasn't meant to be a slap, just the flutter of her hand, like a conductor guiding members of an orchestra, each with the same goal in mind, but different instruments in hand. Mazora Henri, or Toothless Henri, as even the other children with missing teeth called him, had long legs, which he constantly knocked together, and a loud, jumpy laugh.

Of all the children she had ever read to, he interrupted the most, both with his clamorous laugh and by reaching over, whenever her back was turned, to grab, pinch, or shove the other children. Whenever she tried to keep him still, by making him stand alone in the back of the room, he mumbled a long list of audible curse words under his breath. She should have discussed the situation with Max Senior from the beginning, but she had thought herself capable of handling him.

The particular morning of the slap, she was reading out loud to the class a poem called 'Le Soleil et les Grenouilles,' 'The Sun and the Frogs,' by the French fabulist Jean de La Fontaine. Given that the town, like many other coastal towns, no longer had any frogs – something that the French herpetologists had linked to the increased possibility of seismic activity and freak waves – and since the children were already familiar with their parents' or older siblings' accounts of the summer a decade ago when the frogs had disappeared, Louise thought it might be instructive to share the poem, one of her favorites, with them.

As she read aloud, she became completely enthralled, as she did on the radio, with the sound of her own gravelly voice. Rising from the rocking chair, she walked back and forth between the evenly spaced benches, stopping now and then to accentuate a certain part of the poem for a particular row or child.

> . . . Aussitôt on ouït d'une commune voix
> Se plaindre de leur destinée
> Les Citoyennes des Etangs.
> . . . Abruptly, a cry
> From all the frogs in the land
> Who could no longer bear their fate.
> What will we do if the Sun has children?
> We can barely survive one Sun.
> If half a dozen come
> Then the sea will dry up, with all that is in it.
> Farewell, marshes, swamplands: our kind has
>   been destroyed . . .

For a while, she ignored Henri, who was mimicking her facial expressions and lip movements and grimacing to distract the others. But the more Henri was ignored, the more animated his impersonation became, until most of the children stopped listening to laugh at him. Or really to laugh at her.

She couldn't tell when it started, but at some point while she had her back turned, Henri had yanked a ribbon from one girl's hair, then had walked (or jumped) to the next row and pulled a handful of barrettes from Claire Faustin's hair. The sight of Claire's stoic face and the barrettes, spread out now like so many dead aphids on the floor at her feet, enraged Louise, who put the book down and slowly walked toward Henri.

As she approached him, he straightened his body and looked ahead. Even as she was standing beside him, she had not yet decided what to do. Should she send him to the back of the room? Send him home?

She had meant only to accentuate whatever command she gave him by pounding on the notebook in front of him with her open palm. But as she stood before him, a toothless smirk came across his face. She wanted to erase it, the way one might erase words and numbers from a blackboard.

She realized that she'd hit him only when she heard the other children gasp. Henri rubbed the side of his face. There were no finger marks that she could see, no blood streaming past his lips. He didn't cry. Instead, he went on smiling, his toothless gap growing wider, until Louise walked back to her desk and continued reading.

That night, Max Senior left her house without saying a word. It was likely that he wouldn't even speak to her again unless she attended the meeting with the boy's mother and all of this was resolved.

Louise spent the next morning in bed, writing. She had been wrong to hit the boy, she knew, but it wasn't the end of the world. He needed it. In fact he deserved it. This is what she planned to tell his mother. Or maybe she wouldn't. This, she knew, was what was worrying Max Senior the most: that she might not show any remorse.

He was finally letting her go. She sensed this, though he'd not said it out loud. Now she would no longer have the children to read to, including that devil of a boy Henri. And that luminous child Claire. Now she would not even have Max Senior. She had long felt him slipping away, the intrigue of her biblical affliction waning as she moved deeper into middle age.

In the beginning, he had liked the taste of blood in her mouth. He would describe it to her in great detail as though his tongue were not inside *her* mouth.

'It is salty,' he would say. Then he would add, 'It is sweet.' He was convinced that the taste was based on her moods, and she would let him go on and on about it, expressing the same thoughts with different words. And she would daydream of other things as he spoke and she would daydream of how free she would feel without this affliction and she would marvel at how some things could destroy a person's life, like being housebound for a few days when you were bleeding out of your mouth and you had trouble remembering when you had not. And all of a sudden, the past was your haven and the time you felt freest was when you least understood your body, when you were like Henri Désir's favorite victims, when you were a little girl. And this is one of the reasons that Henri Désir had to be stopped. Because boys like him became anguish-causing men, men who felt like they could freely ravage and maim, and they had to be stopped. This is why she would never regret slapping him. She would even slap him again, even more purposefully this time, if she had the chance.

*

Odile and her son were in Max Senior's office that afternoon, just as he said they would be. Sometimes when Louise walked into a place like that, a place bursting with old things – dusty ledgers and educational manuals, creaky desks and chairs, things that could easily be fixed or changed or discarded but were kept as if out of a nostalgic reverence for the past – she felt as though she too were a relic. Everything was old in that room except the boy, Henri.

Max Senior was sitting behind his cracked desk. He seemed relieved to see her, letting out a loud sigh when she came in. Again Odile was wearing her uniform and apron. It was as though she wanted to show the entire town that she had a job. She and her son were sitting across from Max Senior in a pair of tall wicker chairs, one of the boy's feet hanging off the edge. An extra chair had been brought in for Louise and had been placed halfway between them.

Max Senior appeared torn between his roles, his eyes swerving back and forth to look at each of them. Louise could see that he was choosing his words carefully. Finally he simply said, 'Allons. Let's begin.'

Odile sprang up and massaged her buttocks, where the chair had left a damp sweat crease. Louise also rose up from her chair and then Max Senior did too.

Everyone was standing now except Henri, who gripped the sides of his chair with clenched fists while tapping his sneakers against one of the footholds without making any noise.

'Madame?' Odile took a few hesitant steps toward Louise. 'They say you slapped my son?'

Odile kept moving closer, until Louise could feel and smell Odile's warm breath on her face, could almost describe, if pressed, what she had eaten for lunch.

Odile reached toward Henri's chair and, without taking her eyes off Louise, grabbed him by the shoulders and plopped him between herself and Louise. He was, she observed with a cool disinterest, uncharacteristically obedient, flaccid; his arms hung limply at his sides.

'My son has always told me,' Odile said, 'what a good person you are. He told me you are like none of the teachers here, that even if we are poor, you treat him like all the other children and that you have read many wonderful things to him. I said to myself, "My son has much to learn from this woman, this big, famous woman." Am I telling a lie, son?' Odile grabbed her son's chin and pushed his face forward, toward them. Henri shook his head no. His mouth was closed, but his lips trembled, and it seemed to Louise that, for the first time since she'd been around him, he might start to cry.

'Let's all sit down now,' Max Senior said, his fingers drumming his desk.

'You see, Msye.' Odile turned her attention now to Max Senior. 'I know your school does not strike children. I was told this the first day you accepted him here. I am a poor woman. Still you accepted him. I thank you for that. But I can't thank you for the rest. If my son did something wrong,

I would give you permission. I would put my cross on a paper, if I have to, to let you punish him the proper way. But I would never let anyone slap my son on his face, like he was some type of chimè, some brigan, or some criminal. Non, non. That is not correction. It is humiliation.'

Odile now gently took Henri's hand and moved him aside. Freed, he buried his face behind one of the chairs. Stepping back, Odile took a deep breath, then aimed for Louise.

The slap landed on Louise's cheek before she could see it coming. Her head swung so fast that each of her ears tapped against each of her shoulders for a moment. Her cheek throbbed. It felt hot, then warm, then deadened, so that if Odile slapped her again, she probably wouldn't feel a thing. Yet the most painful thing about it was that it felt as though the slap had come from Max Senior. It was as if he had hit her.

'Finished now,' Odile said to both her and Max Senior. 'No more hitting talk. Just teach my child. And remember, correction, not humiliation.'

Odile grabbed Henri's hand and yanked him toward the door. On his way out, with the contented look of the vindicated, Henri turned to face Louise, opened his mouth, and flashed her the gap between his front teeth: his version of a celebratory smile.

Louise heard herself breathing loudly as she tried to massage some sensation back into her cheekbone. The old office door squeaked behind Odile and Henri as they moved into the yard.

Max Senior slipped back into the ancient chair behind

his desk and motioned for Louise to also sit down. His gaze was fixed on her as though, she imagined, he was thinking of the two of them alone in one of those dark rooms of his childhood on those 'Ki moun sa a?' nights, those 'Who are you?' nights, and was trying to figure out who she really was.

She was Louise George. That's who she was. She had always done her best to protect herself from insults and injuries like this. Only for him had she let her guard down with these children, and look where it had led her, into a pitch-black moment of her own.

A droning sound was ringing in her ears, but she thought she heard him ask, 'T'es bien? Are you okay?'

'Why did you let her do that?' She pressed her palm against her cheek and massaged it in a gentle circular motion.

'After so many years of friendship,' he said, 'you think I would tell her to do that to you?' Still, he seemed neither shocked nor outraged, and he did not get up from his chair and walk over to console her.

No matter what he said, she found it hard to believe that he did not approve of that woman slapping her. Odile must have sensed it too. Otherwise she would have never taken the chance. She would have never risked her child getting kicked out of the school, or worse.

Louise was feeling a bit dizzy now. The sound of Max Senior's creaking chair echoed inside her head, his voice drifting in and out of her ears. Why didn't he slap her himself? she wondered.

He no longer wanted her in his life or at the school. She had felt it for some time, but she hadn't been absolutely certain of it. He now turned to look at one of his old wooden cabinets, bursting with years of student dossiers and records. 'The school is my whole life now,' he said, 'and it has to be done right.'

She had heard him go on about all of this before. Here, at the school, he could still nurse and guide childhoods without taking full responsibility for their outcomes. The children were not his children. He could not fully blame himself for their lack of self-possession, their selfishness and failures, their willingness to ruin their lives and the lives of others. But he could at least shield them while they were still young and in his care.

'Even though this is my school,' he said, 'my son, when he was this boy Henri's age, was often misunderstood by the teachers here. And though they never slapped him physically, they often slapped him with words. This is why I would never allow something like you've done here.'

'We are not talking about your son!' she shouted.

'There is such a thing as a social contract then,' he said.

'I did not deserve to be slapped,' she said.

'Neither did that boy.' He pushed his chair forward in her direction, increasing the screeching noise coming from it.

'You didn't even explain to his mother,' she said. 'You didn't even try to help her see my side.'

'You have no side here,' he said. 'Besides, you were not there every moment I was with her.'

'So why was the other man there last night, that man Faustin?'

'Because,' he said, 'as I heard it from the other children, Henri struck his daughter. I was hoping you would be brave enough to reassure both of those people that their children were still safe with us.'

'Then you should have had the whole class there last night,' she said, 'because that boy has hit every one of those children.'

'That may be,' he said. 'But—'

'So this was a konplo,' she said, cutting him off. 'A plot to humiliate *me*?'

'Don't be dramatic, Louise,' he said. 'We are not on your show here.' And the way he twisted his mouth and curled his lips reminded her how much he hated her show.

This might just be an elaborate send-off, she thought. She herself might have chosen a simpler way to say good-bye. But this was Maxime Ardin we were talking about here. Maxime Ardin père, le premier, senior. The son was fils, deux, junior. Maxime Ardin, Sr., did not know of any simple ways to say good-bye. And when he couldn't divorce or banish you, unless you were one of his students, he apparently had you smacked.

'If I did what you did,' he said, while looking so on edge that his teeth were nibbling on his bottom lip, 'I would remove myself from my position. I couldn't continue here.'

He got up, sat down, got up, then sat down again, but did not make an approach toward her. That dreaded feeling of loneliness she felt so often returned.

'Now you can have more time for your show,' he said. Again she noticed his scowl of disdain, for the show and now also for her. He had told her many times that she could have been a great teacher and that the show had kept her from it. But now he knew that she could never be that kind of teacher, and there was no longer much to admire.

'You can also keep writing your book,' he was saying. The slap he'd assigned to another woman was also meant to propel her toward this other redeemable talent, the writing of her book.

One of his favorite things to say to her was that she was like a starfish, that she constantly needed to have a piece of her break off and walk away in order for her to become something new. Of course this had always been truer of him than of her.

As she turned around to leave his office, she saw what he thought he was trying to slap back to life, a stronger and freer woman, one he could both salvage and admire. This slap, she knew, he perversely considered a gift to her, a convoluted act of kindness.

Anniversary

THE NIGHT GAËLLE LAVAUD'S HUSBAND DIED, she thought that everyone should die. After Laurent's murder outside Radio Zòrèy, she'd sold their house in town and moved into her grandparents' house on Anthère Hill. She had turned the fabric shop over to her employees, then had lain in bed for months, also waiting to die. Although everyone said that her milk would be tainted by her sadness and would fill her daughter, Rose, with sadness, Inès, her housekeeper, insisted that Gaëlle nurse her daughter as a way of saving both the child and herself. Gaëlle got out of her bed only when she could no longer keep her daughter in it, when the child began to crawl. And when her daughter started to walk, Gaëlle walked again. And when Rose began to talk, Gaëlle talked again.

She was tempted to close the fabric shop, but she returned to it, because it had meant so much to her husband and, unlike the house, was in a part of town that was less prone to floods, mudslides, and other potential disasters. Business had slowed anyway. People were buying less fabric and more ready-made used clothes, pèpè, from abroad.

She was now mostly selling fabric for school uniforms and even that was dwindling. Besides, during her time of mourning, many of her friendships had dissolved. She no longer attended baptisms, communions, or wedding receptions in the best houses in town. She even refused to listen to broadcasts from the radio station, where her husband had spent so much of his time.

Her husband's murder was never going to be solved. That she knew. There would never be a proper trial. Bribes and corruption would keep anyone from being brought to justice. So she accepted the offer of two Special Forces policemen – childhood friends of both hers and her husband's – to seek another type of justice. And when they had returned from their missions, they'd provided even more details than she had sought. They had walked into a young man's red bedroom, crossed themselves, then shot him dead as he lay in his bed, a young man who used to work at the radio station where her husband had been killed. Later they had returned and set fire to the warehouse the neighborhood gang called home, by spreading gasoline at the entrance, and killed their leader, Tiye, and his second in command. The blaze had spread through the warehouse, then the restaurant next door.

She had not felt the kind of relief she'd expected when she'd heard all this. She hadn't thought that the deaths would bring her husband back, but she'd expected a hole to feel plugged that never was. She likened it to making prints. No matter how long you soaked the cloth in the dye, as long as the fabric was waxed, the color wouldn't change. Little had changed for her. Nothing had been returned to her. A few high-level friendships had made her judge, jury, and executioner. Yet she still felt powerless, incapacitated, cursed.

For a long time, she hadn't ever allowed herself to think about all this, that is, until the day her daughter died. Perhaps it had been no accident, but some terrible cosmic design engulfing everyone involved. Maybe she was not worthy of growing old with the man she had loved most of her life. Or of seeing her daughter grow up. Could it be that there was a puppet master somewhere who despised her and had decided that she was to be made an example of? Had she doomed herself further when she'd turned her rage over to her Special Forces friends? Maybe that's when it was also decided that her daughter's obituary in *La Rosette* would not say that she died after a valiant battle with a long illness.

The driver whose car had struck the motorcycle her daughter was traveling on, sending her only child hurtling into the air to her death, was someone she knew, a young hotelier from a prominent family in town. He was a Moulin.

She had not wanted her daughter to grow up like the Moulins or those other rich kids, who seemed even richer because they lived in a poor town. But she blamed herself every day for not picking Rose up from school that afternoon in her own car.

After Rose died, she would often think back to the first

time she had to leave her for a few hours. It was to attend her husband's funeral. Do you know that feeling when you are about to leave your child and she cries like she will never see you again and you fear that her intense sadness might be some terrible omen? She wished she had never stopped feeling that. She wished she'd seen every simple good-bye as a curse for what she'd done. She wished she'd never let her daughter, not even for one minute, out of her sight.

A few months after Rose died, Inès's eyesight began failing. There were younger people to do the job that she was not doing, Inès had told her, and Inès wanted to spend her last days in her ancestral village in the mountains. Although Inès had been gone for years now, Gaëlle sometimes still craved her company so much that she would wake up in the morning and wait for Inès to come and serve her breakfast, just as she would sometimes wait for her daughter to skip through the doorway and bounce into her bed. At night, after a whole day of watching little girls stream in and out of the fabric shop with their mothers, Gaëlle would imagine Rose as an eight-, then a nine-, now a ten-year-old girl. Her baby teeth would be gone, her baby fat yielding to early prepubescent brawn. Her voice would be more defined, more confident. She would be dressing herself too, picking out her own clothes and combing her own hair. She would be riding a bicycle, swimming in the sea. Her childhood passion for pressing wildflowers into her notebooks would most likely continue. Next to them she might now be pasting cutout magazine photos of film and music stars. Rose would still be getting excellent grades in school – Gaëlle would have seen to that – but would she still want to play with the dozen or so cloth dolls that, ignoring her fancier toys, the two of them had made together? Would she still want to climb up the lighthouse steps and look down at the sea? Would she still want to dance, along with her friends, in their school's maypole dance at Carnival time, or wear the same feathered hat with her Taino costume for the children's parade? Would she still want to fly kites on Saturday after-noons, then go down and watch the fishermen's children launch their miniature boats on the water and run along the beach behind them, chasing the plastic bucket covers they used as Frisbees? Would she still want to know what heaven was and what her father was doing there? Would she still push her head back now and then and shout 'Papa!' to the clouds, then ask if everyone was in heaven, why there was any need for cemeteries? Why didn't the dead just float up and drift away like balloons?

Gaëlle had filled some of the years since her daughter's death with these types of unanswered questions and with the company of men who were interested in either money or sex or both. Couldn't they tell, she often wondered, that she was a shell, a zombie, just as she had been when she was pregnant with her daughter and was sure that her daugh-ter would be born damaged or dead, just as she had been too during those early days after her husband had died? Couldn't they tell that wherever her husband's and daugh-ter's spirits were was where she longed to be? Only Max

Senior had understood this, because he had listened intently to her story about hiring the Special Forces avengers, while holding her hand.

The night of the vigil for the lost fisherman, Caleb, Gaëlle had been expecting Max Senior and his son for dinner. She had skipped Max Junior's welcome-home party the night before and had chosen instead to invite the younger Ardin, through his father, to her home. But earlier that evening Max Senior had called to cancel, offering no explanation.

Before heading to the fisherman's vigil, Gaëlle's young housemaid, Zette, had left her a plate of fried pork and plantains, which Max Senior had requested as part of his dinner. Gaëlle wolfed down the food while lying in bed, wearing a long silver satin evening gown, which she had intended to wear for dinner with the Ardins, father and son. Her hair, though, was still wrapped in rollers when Max Senior had called. With the wide-paned jalousies of her bedroom windows open, she could see some of the houses lit up on the hill, many of which were occupied only part of the year because their owners lived in the capital or abroad. She could also see the Anthère lighthouse, around which her entire neighborhood had been built.

The lighthouse gallery was filled with young boys, some of whom were fighting with the wind to light hurricane lamps, while others twirled flashlights. Gaëlle's grandfather, her mother's father – a mason and engineer – had built that lighthouse with help from a group of fishermen. Some of those fishermen were still alive, but most were living elsewhere or had died. When a fancy neighborhood – Anthère, named after the anther of a rose – sprang up on the hill, there was little need for the lighthouse, the lights from the homes becoming beacons themselves. The mayor and other town officials had shown no interest in spending to maintain the lighthouse. But it had been constructed so well – with a fifty-foot tower and an equally high focal plane – that it refused to rot.

In the old days, when the lighthouse was functioning, it was painted all white and had a red lamp and a windbreak on top. Her grandfather and the other volunteer light keepers would ensure that the kerosene lamps that fueled the lantern were lit every night at dusk, producing ten flashes per minute. All this she had learned from her grandfather. He would guide her by the hand, up the spiral staircase toward the lighthouse gallery. The air was always damp and stale in the inside chamber, the spaces under the stairs covered with intricate spiderwebs.

Reaching the lighthouse gallery, though, was always her favorite moment. From there, she could see the land, the mountains, and the sea bathed in sun, mist, or fog, depending on the season, or the time of day. Her grandfather would let her pull the lever that would sound the lighthouse foghorn, and she'd scream over the blast, unable to hear her own voice. Every now and then, if she was lucky, they'd see a rainbow. Her grandfather could spot even the faintest band of light in the clouds or distant fog banks.

But now the lighthouse was placed in rescue mode only when someone was missing, or in remembrance mode when someone was dead. The paint on the outside had long since faded, leaving the cement and rocks exposed. The lantern too was long gone. Battered by wayward birds, it had been crashed into so many times that it had collapsed. Before that the lamp had been infested by bats. The foghorn had also disappeared, removed, she suspected, by someone or a group of someones who'd found a better use for it. She'd not been inside for so long that she didn't know what shape the staircase was in, but the fact that so many people were always in there meant it must be holding up well.

As she watched the lights flicker from the gallery she'd loved so much, she told herself that she should fix the lighthouse. She should have it repaired and equipped with modern gadgets, a solar panel or something that would make it operate on its own. Placing her empty plate on the nightstand by her bed, she decided that she would offer a lighthouse, restored, to the town as a gift and would officially reopen it with a massive celebration.

She rose from her bed and walked to another room in the house, one that was furnished like all the others, with a canopy bed, an armoire, and a woven rug the same color as the drapes. From there she could see dozens of people pacing from one end of the beach to the other, as though hoping that they would be the ones to find the lost fisherman.

Watching the bonfire from yet another room, the room she'd imagined would be her daughter's one day, when her daughter stopped sleeping with her, Gaëlle stepped out on the wide terrace that made that room the second-best one in the house. She first felt a chill and wrapped her arms around her body, but soon she forgot about it, concentrating instead on the voices swirling around her in an uninterrupted murmur, some coming from the lighthouse and some from the beach.

Already she was trying to forget her vow to repair the lighthouse. How do you even choose what to mend when so much has already been destroyed? How could she think, she asked herself, that she could revive or save anything?

Her thoughts returned to Max Senior and his son not coming to dinner. She'd been counting on it so much, as a way of filling up a few more hours in this awful day, as a way of making it mean something else, if only for a short while. It helped, after visiting her husband's and daughter's graves, to take part in these normal types of activities on this day, to pretend for a few short hours that she was no longer hurting as much as the year before.

Her daughter had been a student at École Ardin, Max Senior's school. Last year, on the anniversary of her daughter's death, after attending their friend Albert's mayoral inauguration, and after a meeting with the fisherman Nozias about his daughter and deciding not to take her, and after Max Senior had grown tired of the Anthère Hill fireworks celebration party, they had spotted each other at Pauline's, a popular bar with an upstairs brothel on the outskirts of town. The dim, smoke-clouded speakeasy was run by another old friend of theirs, a cross-eyed Canadian bar-tender in his late fifties. She'd been wearing a white hibiscus behind her left ear. The flower had caressed Max Senior's cheek when she kissed him hello. The kiss lingered awhile, which seemed to surprise him, and he asked if she was alone. She said yes and he said he was now too, but was only there to have a drink.

When it was time for her to leave, she reached up again to kiss him, this time on the lips. After their lips parted, he raised his hand to the spot and traced her mouth's outline on top of his. They became linked by that kiss, and soon he started visiting her at her house.

He was an inconsistent lover, and she even thought he might be sleeping with someone else. She would see him once or twice a week, but never more than that.

'I know today is an infinitely difficult day for you,' he'd said earlier on the phone, just as he had that night a year ago, at the bar.

'Every day is an infinitely difficult day for me,' she'd replied.

That first night after they'd made love, she'd told him that she was going to find a man to marry, that she'd convince that man to take her away, to Port-au-Prince, or even to another country. There were too many memories in this town to bind her and make her want to flee at the same time.

'No one will ever love you more than you love your pain,' he had replied, his words ringing even louder in the dark.

She had not understood what he meant at first, but eventually it occurred to her that he might be right. Her pain, her losses: these were what was keeping her in this town. His grasping this, his understanding of it, made him seem even more appealing, more powerful. This momentary ability to comfort her made them all seem powerful: the Special Forces policemen, the bartenders, the Max Seniors, these men who seemed able to fully exist in the world, something that she wished she could extract from them.

Looking down at a row of bougainvilleas beneath her terrace, Gaëlle ran her fingers across her lips just as, at the beginning of their affair, Max Senior had so often done. This house, with all its creaking wood and empty spaces, often drove her to desperate gestures. Whenever Zette or the yardman was away, she felt the full weight of being alone. The only children of only children often end up with no kin. This had always been her husband's argument for the three other children they had intended to have.

Gaëlle stepped into her slippers, then walked out of the house, with every intention of walking down to the beach. But then she saw next to her husband's rusting old Cabriolet the new, boxy white Mercedes that she had bought, wishing that they'd had something like it when he was alive. With Elie, the genius town mechanic, keeping it going, she had driven the Cabriolet until a year ago, when it, like everything else, had died.

Running back to her room, she grabbed her keys from her purse. She thought of changing out of the evening gown, of removing the rollers from her hair, of exchanging the slippers for shoes, but decided against it.

Pauline's was nearly empty, except for a few men who'd come to see the girls who were upstairs in the brothel section of the place. Her bartender friend was at his station, and rather than sit in the restaurant with the waiting men, she sat on one of the wooden stools across from him. He reached over the bar and wrapped her shoulders in a tight alcohol-scented embrace. Someone was watching them from one of the tables on the other side of the empty dance floor, a muscular, olive-skinned man with a full beard. He looked young and sophisticated in spite of his beard, while his expensive shirt, the type with the designer's name emblazoned in sequined writing on the back, proclaimed that he had money. He was the kind of man the girls would fight over in a place like this, the kind they would assume could detect that they weren't all common, that some had even been educated, to whatever extent possible, by their families. Some of them had gone as far as university, but for financial reasons had not been able to either finish or find any other type of work.

On her regular visits to the bar at Pauline's, Gaëlle had seen very pretty girls present themselves in pairs, trios, and quartets to men like this. In her fancy body-hugging evening gown and rollers, she might have been mistaken by the young man for one of the older house girls, or even their madam, on a break.

'Who's that?' she asked the bartender.

'That's Yves Moulin,' he said, quickly placing a glass of red wine in front of her and sharing her apparent agony at hearing the name. 'With that beard and all the weight he's been lifting,' he added, 'it's like he's got a bag over his head.'

Yves Moulin was the young man whose car had hit the motorcycle her daughter had been riding on. His family owned a popular hotel between Ville Rose and Cité Pendue. Before the accident, Yves Moulin had been a star in the youth soccer league in Ville Rose and everyone thought that he'd be recruited by a team in Europe. But after the accident he gave up playing altogether and stayed mostly in the private residence at the hotel. People said he was unable to get the image of her daughter out of his mind, of her daughter's body taking off from the back of the motorcycle and seeming to fly. They speculated that he couldn't separate this image from that of kicking a soccer ball. The ball too was flying. And it was his foot that was refusing to let it rest on the ground.

The way the town gossip mill was able to make his private nightmares public made her wonder what kinds of stories they told about her. What kinds of words had they placed on her lips? No matter what he'd lost, or how much regret he'd shown, no matter that every year on the anniversary of the accident Yves Moulin placed a small bouquet of white roses at her daughter's gravesite, each rose for one year of the age that her daughter would have been, had she lived, no matter that he had tried to show that he too remembered her daughter, still, she could not forgive him.

Her eyes met his across the empty dance floor. He looked at her, then his eyes wandered toward the front entrance, as though he were searching for an escape.

She hadn't seen or heard from him since he'd come to her house the day after her daughter's death to offer to pay the funeral expenses. Her parents, who'd come from Port-au-Prince for the services, had turned him away at the door, and he kindly had not returned. He had done a good job of making himself scarce, until now. Or it could be that she had seen him and not recognized him. Sometimes she would think she saw him, in a crowd or from a distance, but the next second he would disappear, making her wonder if thinking she saw him was like those times when she thought she saw her daughter too.

'Looks like he wants to say hello to you,' the bartender murmured.

And before Gaëlle could climb down from the stool and flee, Yves Moulin was standing right in front of her, less than an arm's length away.

'Bonsoir,' he said. His body was large, imposing, his voice deeper.

When she did not answer, he turned around and walked back to the table where he'd been sitting. He downed his half-finished drink in one swift move and left.

Soon after, a few of the girls came downstairs to say

good-bye to one customer and greet another. The bartender offered Gaëlle a more potent drink than wine. Mixing portions from the contents of several containers, he slid a tall, colorful concoction toward her. The drink numbed her the way she'd hoped it would, enough to give her enough courage to get back into her car and head to the beach.

Driving the shortcuts and back roads, the épines, as she watched the cloud of insects the car's headlights were attracting, she couldn't help but think that had the bartender not told her who Yves Moulin was, she might have possibly walked over to his table and offered herself to him. On this night, like so many others, he might have ended up being just one more kind face, one more comforting voice, one more set of arms to be wrapped around her body. He wouldn't have had to say much. What he did say, 'Bonsoir,' might have been enough. The sad thing was that she was foolishly thinking it might still be possible. She wondered whether their coming together in this way – to love rather than kill – might resolve everything at last. Might her looking down at his sorrowful face, and his being in her sorrowful bed, help them both take back that moment on the road? She would also judge for herself if what everyone said was true, that he was as wounded as she was.

When she finally made it to the beach, she spotted a group of little girls. They were holding one another's hands and moving clockwise in a circle, a singing circle, a wonn. She was too far away to hear what they were singing, but she could hear their laughter, each girl, it seemed, trying to outdo the next. They seemed to be the happiest people in Ville Rose, six little brown and black angels skipping around fallen sea hearts and sand dollars.

She moved slowly, not wanting the pleasure of her approach to end. She had played the wonn as a child, during recess, and at night in her parents' yard, with visiting friends. What she remembered most about it, though, was how less lonely she felt holding someone else's hand.

It would have sounded odd – people have been accused of sorcery for less – if she told someone how much she wanted to take all those little girls home, set them up in the many empty rooms of her house, and, whenever she was sad, ask them to play with her. There were many days when she wanted to grab a little girl and hold her in her arms, just to inhale her smell, the smell that these men lacked. Their smells were musty: they smelled of roads and dust and cologne that never quite covered their musk. They smelled of work, of sweat, of other women. But little girls smelled of roses and wet leaves, of talcum powder, and the dew.

In spite of what Inès and nearly everyone else had told her after her daughter died, longings like this had never subsided. And her losses had not made her stronger; they had made her weak. They had given others control and power over her. She didn't want to continue being weak, but she didn't want to die either. She was too eager to see what would come next, what her husband and daughter had missed. She was both hungry for life and terrified of it. Her evenings with these men let the rage and confusion disappear for a while and allowed her to make it through her days. They allowed her to sell thread and cloth and remain close to the graves of the people she really loved.

There were times, as she'd told Max Senior, that she wanted to take off, leave Ville Rose, leave the country, and never come back. But she'd heard too much about the difficulties of starting a new life in another land to want to try. She'd heard about people who had been infantilized while learning a new language, people who'd ended up cleaning houses or wiping the asses of other people's children. She saw these people return to Ville Rose at Christmas or in the summertime, with extravagant hairstyles and expensive-looking clothes, but their eyes always betrayed them. All the humiliation they had endured could be detected there. Their skins betrayed them too, the burns from the dry cleaner's steamer or the car wash or the restaurant kitchens, as visible as brands on animals. Non, none of that was for her. Her ancestors on both sides were buried at the town cemetery, among the town's oldest families. She could not be dyaspora. She liked her ghosts nearby. She could never live in a foreign land, then return only a few times a year. She could not ever risk dying and being buried in a cold place. She would always be here, she thought, like the boulder that stopped her feet when at last she reached the little girls.

One of the girls, Claire, realized that she was being watched and occasionally glanced her way. Like her mother,

Claire was beautiful. She moved more gracefully, more purposefully, than the rest of the girls, even the ones who were older. Gaëlle walked over to the girls, and immediately her presence stopped the game.

'Do you remember my daughter?' the girl's father, Nozias, often asked Gaëlle when they saw each other.

How could Gaëlle forget a child whom she had nursed as a baby on the very night that she was born, a child who was so gentle, so docile, even on that first day, and had grown so lovely, so radiant, with each passing year?

'Is your papa here?' Gaëlle asked Claire.

The girl nodded; she was looking down at her hands, then at her sand-coated feet. Impatient, the other girls lost interest and drifted away.

Gaëlle motioned for the girl to follow her. Claire sat down next to her and from behind one of the boulders pulled out a pair of rubber sandals. Gaëlle waited for her to finish placing the sandals on her feet, then said, 'I knew your mother.'

Claire's eyes seemed to light up the way children's eyes do when they're hungry for stories.

'I knew her longer than you've been alive,' Gaëlle said. 'Your mother was my friend.'

It was not altogether a lie.

The girl's head was arched toward her, her mouth wide open, as though to inhale Gaëlle's words, which came out so fast that Gaëlle could barely stop. Gaëlle was not sure what she was thinking and what she was saying out loud. 'When your mother was pregnant with you, your mother gave up washing and dressing the dead. Then she had all the time to do nothing but go out on the water with your father and sew. She waited so long to have you, your mother. I wouldn't even say wait. She tried. She tried. She tried to pull you out of the sky, pry you out of God's hands. Yes, God's hands, I'd say. I don't go to church every Sunday. I don't go to church at all, but she wanted you so bad. I know she pulled you out of God's hands. That's the only way I can put it. She was well the whole time you were inside her body. Never even seemed tired when she came into the shop, except the last week, when she didn't come. Then the midwife was sent for. No one knows what happened while you were being born. I hear the midwife thought all was going well. You should not blame yourself. That revenan talk is superstition. Nobody *returns*. That is not real. You're gone. You're gone. Back in God's hands, and no one can pull you back. Not you. Not you, Claire. I hope you understand. Not you back in God's hands, but your mother and my Lòl and my Rosie and your mother too and everyone else who has died who didn't deserve to die. Though who deserves to die? Too many people die here, and why do the rest of us get to live?

'Happy birthday, Claire,' Gaëlle said, both her thoughts and her voice now slowing down.

There was still so much more she wanted to tell the girl, though. She wanted to tell her about seeing her mother at her husband's gravesite service, but this part might be impossible for the girl to grasp. Claire's mother might have even been at the cathedral for her husband's funeral Mass – the whole town, it seemed, was there – but Gaëlle hadn't noticed if she was. But she remembered well seeing Claire's mother at the burial ground, standing near the cemetery gate.

In the normal course of life as a new mother, Gaëlle, according to custom, shouldn't have been outside in the open air at all, for fear that her nouris body – weakened by childbirth – might be too frail. But against everyone's advice, the morning of her husband's funeral Mass and burial service she'd left her infant daughter at home with Inès and attended both. During the gravesite prayers, her breasts ached and swelled, wetting the front of her white dress. She looked beyond the deep hole in the ground, beyond the bronzed coffin, beyond Pè Marignan and the large crowd of townspeople around her, toward the cemetery gate, eager to be at home with her baby. This was when she saw Claire Narcis standing alone under a flame-colored weeping willow by the cemetery gate. Claire Narcis was wearing the same plain black dress she wore to the funerals of all the townspeople whose bodies she had washed and dressed for burial.

That morning, it seemed that Claire Narcis and the weeping willow had become one. Claire's body seemed indistinguishable from the small part of the willow's trunk that was not covered by its drooping branches. Claire's head was topped by the willow's golden crown. Claire Narcis had seemed that morning to be a dazzling mirage, a veil between the dirt being piled on her husband's coffin and the wailing baby waiting at home. And Claire's presence at the cemetery gate, and the surprising way it had both jolted and comforted her, was one of the reasons she'd agreed to nurse Claire's daughter when she was newly born, and one of the many reasons she could honestly call the girl's mother her friend.

Nozias was now standing over Gaëlle and the girl. He plopped himself down next to them, nearly falling over his daughter.

Fòk nou voye je youn sou lòt, Claire Narcis had often told her. Gaëlle put her hands on the girl's back and felt the child's body shaking. She had finally made up her mind. Yes, she would take her.

'Tonight,' she said.

Immediately she began to worry. Maybe she had said too much. Maybe she had upset the child with all that talk. Maybe things were moving too fast.

'Now?' her father asked. 'Tonight?'

He immediately shifted his total attention to Claire, almost as if Gaëlle were no longer there. This surprised her. Hadn't he been trying to give the girl to her for years?

He mentioned something about not changing her name and his having a letter for her, then Claire raised her arms. 'Bagay mwen yo,' she said.

What about her things? Gaëlle wondered.

But the girl did not wait for them to give her permission; she simply turned and started toward their place.

Gaëlle wasn't sure how long it had been, but people

were slipping away and heading home, and the girl had not returned.

'I'll get her,' Nozias said.

Gaëlle watched him head for the shack. He was doing his best to stay upright under the weight of his sadness about seeing his daughter go. He too disappeared inside the shack. Then he walked out, shouting the girl's name.

Gaëlle rushed to his side. She followed him through the alleys between the shacks, then down toward the water, all the while calling the girl's name along with him and his neighbors.

'We should take my car and look for her in town,' she finally said, when it seemed to her that Claire might have left the beach.

'Non,' he replied firmly, as if to put himself back in control. 'She's just hiding. She will come back.' She understood his need to remain in control. Even though he had just given her to him, she was still his child.

'You keep looking,' she said. 'And I will wait at your place for her.'

She followed him to his doorstep. He rushed ahead of her and lit up the small shack, which was the size of one of her terraces. It did not smell like the sea, like it had the last time she was there. It smelled like the long matchstick he had just pounded against the side of the matchbox and the kerosene wick on the hourglass lamp he had just lit. Part of the room was now filled with a flaxen glow, the rest full of shadows. He reached above his cot and unclasped, then pushed open, the flaps of a small window, letting some air in and some smoke out. Then he closed the flaps just as quickly. He seemed nervous, scared even, but was doing his best not to let her see it.

Gaëlle tried very hard to not, once again, confuse her heartache with desire. Still, she thought she'd give him a hint of her temptation by sitting on his cot.

He walked out.

He left anyway.

Di Mwen, Tell Me

'TELL ME, FLORE VOLTAIRE,' Louise George was saying, her gaunt body erect, her spine ruler straight, behind the studio microphone. 'We are ready to hear your story.'

'There was a hailstorm . . . ,' Flore began, closing her eyes to avoid looking directly at Louise's bony face.

There was a hailstorm the night Max Ardin, Jr., came to Flore Voltaire's bed. The ice balls, tiny at first, were pounding the roof of the first-floor room attached to the kitchen. It was a narrow room, the smallest one in Max Senior's house, perhaps built for someone who was spending the night but not staying for long, as Flore and her aunt, the previous maid, had.

Exhausted from a long day of cleaning and preparing dinner, Flore was flipping through a beauty magazine that she'd found lying around in the living room when the thumping on the roof grew louder. The sequined dresses, long legs and necks, and high-heeled shoes she was idly studying made her beige polyester night slip feel even flimsier, older, and uglier, but she kept flipping the pages anyway.

She had been in hailstorms before, in Cité Pendue.

Sometimes during these storms, a house not as sturdy as this one would be pummeled so badly that it would be blown over by the winds that followed.

The lights were out all over Max Senior's house, and Max Junior seemed to be just wandering around with a flashlight when he came into her room. At first she thought he'd come for the magazine, so she quickly handed it to him, ashamed of her stargazing at long hair and made-up faces. He took the magazine from her without saying a word – not even hello – and he left. She pulled the door closed behind him, turning the small lock. It was not the first time he'd been in her room. It was his father's house, after all. Those times, he would come to ask her where something was, or to put something together, a sandwich or some tea, for him or his father. But that night, she sensed, was different. He seemed lost.

She walked back to her bed and lay down on her side, raising the blanket over her body, all the way up to her neck, as she'd slept most of her life. She could then hear the footsteps approaching. He was returning. The lock was no use. The door, it seemed, was made to be opened easily. He walked over and sat on the edge of her bed. The sound of the hail seemed to grow more and more distant until it stopped entirely, giving way to the patter of rain and the occasional sparks of thunder and lightning.

He said nothing. She closed her eyes and tried to pretend he wasn't there. Then she opened her eyes again and looked around, her gaze settling on the flashlight illuminating his blank, vacant face. Underneath his shave coat, he was naked.

At first she thought he was asleep, sleepwalking, dreaming on his feet. Or that she was. She was too frightened to speak. The lightning and thunder did not seem to trouble him, and he moved his face toward hers until her body was pinned beneath his on the bed. He was heavy, twice the size of most nineteen-year-olds. She thought this had something to do with his having done his secondary and university schooling locked up in his father's office at École Ardin, getting lessons from his old man. He had never, as her mother liked to say, even been sprinkled by the rain.

As he pulled her night slip up toward her chest, she thought she saw a few drops of rain in a corner of the room, sliding down the walls from the ceiling. Maybe the roof had been damaged in the hailstorm. And if the roof were damaged, then she was no safer inside than she would be outside.

When he left the room – was it some minutes or hours or days later? – the rain was still falling, though not as heavily as before. She walked out into the courtyard rose garden, next to the pool, raising her face to the sky. The wind rattled her, her body soaked.

When she went back to the room, she saw that he'd left his flashlight behind. It was still on. She aimed the light at her drenched face, in her confusion thinking somehow that it might have the same effect as a mirror, allowing her to see her eyes. She left the flashlight on and laid it on the floor outside her door in case he should return for it. There was no point in locking the door – she knew that now.

The rain kept on falling with a persistence that made

it seem it would last forever. Slipping back under her blanket, she felt the torment of the fabric scraping her skin. She could still feel the danger brewing both inside and outside the house, the scorched smell of lightning cracking open the surrounding palms and the echoes of swelling waves meeting the seashore. She imagined water pouring underneath the door, after rising over the flashlight, quenching its light, and carrying it away. It would be warm water, filled with leaves. She imagined seeing, as she had in other floods, fire-red ants floating in fist-size balls on the water's surface. The house would then dislodge from the earth, and she would open the door and peek outside and the water would be like a black sheet all around her and she would not see land for miles.

She felt a stabbing pain in places where he had pummeled his body against hers. She had used all her weight to try to push him off of her, but could not. She had tried to slap his hands off of her, as though they were cloying animals, leeches or a jellyfish. He still had not spoken, was not making any sounds. He had been swimming earlier that evening and still smelled like the sea.

The house had rocked as his entire body covered hers, but the house had shaken before, during other storms. What was new was the water coming up so fast, with fire ants, which meant that it was coming down from deep inside the mountains and the hills, and not the sea. She smelled rum on his breath. She gasped for her own breath.

The next morning the sun seemed to rise even earlier

than usual, as if in defiance of all that had taken place the night before. Flore looked through a crack in the door and saw him and his father emerge from the orchid nursery by the gazebo in the middle of the garden. A hummingbird flew over the pummeled rosebushes, and Max Junior raised his fingers, as if to grab the minute wings. Both men looked solemn and stone-faced, their eyes focused on the hail-crushed flowers, as they inspected the storm damage.

While they were in the garden, Flore walked out of the house and took a taxi to Cité Pendue. The traffic, detoured from flooded areas, crawled, her bones throbbing with every lurch and sway of the car.

When she got to her mother's house, her mother was not there.

She opened the door and waited inside. She was feeling too dirty to sit on her mother's plastic-covered chairs. Instead she sat on the cool cement floor.

Her mother was a short but robust woman. When she finally walked in, she was carrying on top of her head a large wicker basket filled with aluminum bowls and cups that she used to sell breakfast foods at the market. As she approached Flore, her mother's lips were rounded as though she were whistling.

When her mother got close enough, Flore helped her mother lower the basket from her head and place it on the floor. Before Flore could say anything, her mother made her stoop down again and, looking at Flore's tear-swollen face, she traced her fingers over Flore's cheek.

'If you're home for good,' her mother said, 'I don't know how we'll get by.'

Flore pulled herself up, reached into her dress pocket, and handed her mother the month's salary that she'd hoped to use for her escape. Then she returned to the Ardins that afternoon, in time to cook their supper.

'You mean to tell me you went back there, back to the Ardins?' Louise finally interrupted Flore now as they taped her show.

Louise was dressed that morning in one of her signature A-line mauve dresses, her hair pulled back tightly, her chin pointed, her eyes narrowed, focused. She was determined to extract the entire story from Flore, along with every detail that she considered necessary. 'Di mwen,' she said. 'Tell me, tell everyone why you went back to the Ardins that afternoon. But first, a commercial break.'

There were no commercials played during the actual taping. They waited just a few minutes as Louise took a sip of water from one of the two glasses in front of them, then said to Flore, 'Relax – you're doing well.'

Flore raised her eyes from her intertwined fingers and looked around the studio, a square room not unlike the one she had slept in at Max Senior's. On the triangular table were two microphones and the water glasses, Louise's now only half full. Louise had bypassed the headphones, offering the ones she usually used to Flore's son.

Pamaxime was sitting underneath the table at his mother's feet, taking turns doodling with a pencil and pad Louise had given him and quietly playing a game on Flore's cell phone. Flore's eyes traveled between her son's headphone-covered ears and the man sitting at the large control board on the other side of the glass, but she made every effort to avoid looking at Louise George, the fierce but tiny hostess of the program.

Flore now picked up the glass of water that was meant for her and took a sip from it. She had called the station and asked for Louise George as soon as she'd learned from Max Senior that his son was coming home and that he wanted to meet the boy.

This was the premise of these personal interviews, Louise had explained to her – you are talking about one moment that changed your life. A moment that made everything that had come before it seem meaningless. A moment that had transformed you inside and out. That night in the maid's room with Max Junior on top of her had been that moment for Flore. Beyond that, Louise had explained, you had to name names, and in this particular case the names had to be repeated as often as possible. Those whose names were mentioned on the program, those who were accused, could always come on her show the following week to defend themselves.

Flore initially had no trouble with the naming, but she was now finding it difficult to go on with the rest of her story. Even though Louise had allowed her to record the show early in the morning – to be aired later that evening and a few more times during the following week – Flore could not forget that her son was right there, sitting at both their feet, under the table, and although he was wearing headphones, Pamaxime might still be able to hear.

'These commercial breaks take up a big chunk of the hour,' Louise said as she prepared to start again. 'And they are long. But what can you do?'

The man at the control board on the other side of the glass signaled to them to continue.

'Go on, tell me.' Louise moved even closer now, their cheeks almost touching. 'Tell me what happened next,' she urged.

'I became pregnant with his baby,' Flore continued in a steely voice that had long replaced the girlish voice she'd once had, the sound of which she could no longer remember.

This interview was good preparation for what was coming, Flore thought, for seeing Max Junior later that same morning. She wanted her son to see him too, if only this one time. Flore was curious to experience for herself how she would hold up in front of Max Junior. There would be no more tears, though. If anything, she would now do everything possible to drive him and his father to tears, with this show. Thankfully, she and Louise seemed to have similar goals.

'By his baby, you mean Maxime Ardin, Jr.'s baby?' Louise pressed her.

Flore nodded.

'This is not television,' Louise said. 'You have to speak.'

These little remarks in the middle of a painful story

always made people in the listening audience laugh. Sometimes, while sitting in her house writing, on those nights that her show aired, Louise could hear laughter erupt from an entire row of houses. She never even had to turn on her own radio. She could hear the show blasting simultaneously from dozens of houses, and during those moments she felt she was the most powerful person in town. Her only regret was that due to the station's limited capacities, the show aired only in Ville Rose and a few surrounding towns, not all over the country.

'Yes,' Flore continued, as if having paused for the expected laughter from the television remark.

Louise turned dead serious again. 'I still don't understand why you went back. Why would you go back there after something like this had been done to you?'

The words had not come out as clearly as Flore had hoped. She wanted to explain how her mind had been all mixed up that night after he had appeared in her room, how she hadn't been quite sure whether or not she was dreaming.

'Why would you go back?' Louise insisted.

'I could not lose my job,' was all that came out now.

'Are those the only choices you had?' Louise asked her. 'Couldn't you have gone to the commissariat and filed a complaint?'

Somewhere in the audience, Louise knew, someone would chuckle. Probably many would. What good would it have done to have filed a police complaint against Max Senior's son? A few dollars to some low- or high-level police official would get Max Junior off. Case in point, one of Max Senior's best friends was the current mayor.

The audience would be aware that Louise was playing devil's advocate, and when Louise played devil's advocate the listeners enjoyed the show even more.

Flore answered the question anyway. 'Tell me, how many people in my situation get justice?'

Louise scratched her gaunt chin and paused to ponder this. She moaned so that the audience might hear and take part in her contemplation.

'Couldn't you have found another job?'

'I am – was – paying,' Flore said, 'the rent for my mother's house.'

'I'm sure your mother understood that you were in a bad situation and would have liked for you to get out,' Louise countered.

Flore's feet jerked so fast that the sound of her knees hitting the table could be heard when the show aired. 'If that is the way you want to see it,' she said.

Just then her son's hands brushed against her calf. When she looked down, she saw the back of his neck and his hands as he placed his pencil to the pad Louise had given him to start his drawing.

'When did you realize that you had become pregnant?' Louise continued.

'I realized I was pregnant a few weeks later, when I started vomiting,' Flore said. She looked down and made sure the headphones were tightly wrapped around her son's ears, then added, 'The vomiting was so bad that I sometimes vomited in the food I was preparing for them.'

Louise would be able to feel that question pulse through her listeners' minds later on. She anticipated the collective gasp that would rise all over town. Has my servant been vomiting in my dinners? some would ask themselves.

They paused for another commercial break. Louise was smiling, the dark lines between her teeth showing. Flore looked down to check on her son, who seemed actively engaged in both doodling on Louise's pad and tapping the keys on the cell phone very softly, as he had been admonished not to do. Flore couldn't see what her son had drawn on the page because the phone and his hands were covering it.

When they started again, Louise asked, 'Who did you first tell that you were pregnant?'

'I told the father first,' Flore continued.

'You mean not your son's father. You mean Maxime Ardin, Sr.?' Louise asked.

'Yes,' Flore answered.

'The owner and headmaster of École Ardin?'

'Li menm.'

'You told him first?'

'Wi.'

'And tell me, what did Maxime Ardin, Sr., say when you told him?'

'He said he couldn't know that this was his son's child. Then he gave me two thousand dollars American from him and his wife, to disappear, to go away.'

'Two thousand dollars U.S., which converts into sixteen thousand dollars Haitian or eighty thousand gourdes, from the father who's here and the mother who's in Miami, to disappear. Is that the going rate?' Louise let out a purposefully forceful laugh to make her point.

So much for Max Senior's righteous indignation. It was just like him to make up his own rules for everything. She should have slapped him back after he'd made that woman slap her.

Louise imagined heads nodding all over town when her audience heard about the two thousand American dollars. That wasn't so bad, some might mutter. Another family might have just thrown her out and not given her anything at all.

'I took that money and I did leave,' Flore went on. 'I went to Port-au-Prince to live with one of my mother's cousins, and while waiting for my son to be born, I started a business.'

Beauty had always fascinated Flore. She found it as resilient as wozo, the colorful weeds and wildflowers that grew, despite being regularly trampled, in the muck beside rivers and back roads. She liked to see women perfectly coiffed and garbed in elegant-looking, even if cheap, dresses. She believed that even the poorest and unhappiest of women could fight heartache with beauty, with bright or muted kerchiefs, head wraps, or hats, relaxed or braided hair, wigs, and talcum-powdered necks. Even while sitting across from Louise, Flore thought that Louise could look prettier if she did more than pull back her hair, which made her face look so severe. She thought that Louise could use some lipstick in a pale shade and a black dot from an eyeliner pencil as a beauty mark.

'What kind of business did you start?' Louise asked.

'A beauty parlor,' Flore said.

Louise imagined cheers erupting all over town. 'Even in their misery,' Louise purred into the microphone, 'our women try to be beautiful.'

This was Louise's favorite part of the show, the part where the horrible story began to take a positive turn. It was the equivalent of a first goal during an impossible soccer match, the moment where everything changes, if only for one side. This is why she was glad that this story had been plucked from the town rumor mill and landed on her lap, why she was thrilled, overjoyed, that this young woman had sought her out. That and to return Max Senior's slap to him. No, she was not a turn-the-other-cheek kind of gal, and in that moment in his office, Max Senior had forced her to be. She believed in an eye for an eye, and though she had never used the show for revenge in the past, she was not above doing it.

'The beauty parlor grew fast.' Flore was catching her stride now, stammering and hesitating less. 'We made a lot of women beautiful,' she said.

'And you?' Louise asked. 'How were you changed?'

This is what had kept *Di Mwen* on the air all these years. This is why people loved the show. She always looked for the pot of gold at the end of her guests' rainbows.

'Well, I'm still here,' Flore said, relieved that the program seemed to be drawing to a close. 'Nou la.'

Finally, the closing question, which Louise asked of every guest, in part to cover herself, to show that these people had sought her out and not the other way around. The question showed, or at least made it appear, that all she did was offer them a platform, to tell their stories themselves, that there was no ill intent on her part, nothing in it for her.

'Why did you come on *Di Mwen*?' she asked Flore. 'Why did you want to get this off your chest?'

'With all their money, even after the way he came to be, they could take my son away from me,' Flore said in her most defiant voice yet. 'As if they could say I am not worthy of him.'

'The Ardins. Father and son, you mean?'

'Yes, them.'

'They want to take your child from you?'

'I won't let them.'

'So what do you do now?' Louise asked.

'I am going far away,' Flore said, pausing to further consider the possibility.

'I suppose you can't tell me where.'

'Non.'

'You told me that Maxime Ardin, Sr., and his wife had given you money for the child.'

'Wi.'

'And you have put that money into your beauty business?'

'Yes.'

'Will it be hard to live without that money?'

'It will be harder to live without my son.'

'So, just to be clear, you are taking your son with you?'

'My mother and my son are coming with me, yes,' Flore said. 'They will never see us again. I am here to tell them to never look for us again, because they will never find us. Even when I am dead and my son is a grown man, I will be sure they never find him. He will have a different name. He will be a different kind of man—'

This seemed a good place for Louise to close, without forcing her guest to compromise her plans and offer hints as to where she would end up. They had only a few seconds left anyway, so Louise had to interrupt her to have the final word.

'Thank you, Flore Voltaire, for sharing your story with us,' she said. Then, in a dramatically grave voice, she added, 'I hope you achieve your goal and find the right place for you and your child.'

Soon after the recorder was turned off, Flore removed the headphones from her son's ears, but it turned out that the boy had been – as nearly everyone in town would later be – glued to every word. He looked up at her and smiled a toothy smile of both confusion and pride at what he'd understood: that he was now going to meet his father, before going someplace far away.

Louise took the headphones from Flore, then held out her hand for the child to return the pad he'd been drawing on.

'Let's see.' Louise looked at the stick figure on the pad. It was obviously meant to be a person, possibly a man, since the boy had not drawn hair or a skirt. The man had no eyes, nose, or mouth, the outline of his face a simple 0. Searching for some hint of what the boy meant by his drawing, Louise smiled at him and guessed out loud. 'A goat?' she asked, teasing the boy.

He laughed, covering his mouth with his hands, then answered, 'Non.'

'A cow?'

'Non.'

'Me?' Louise ventured.

'Papa mwen,' the boy said. 'My father.'

'Write "Papa,"' Louise recommended.

The boy wrote the word *papa*, the tiny letters spread wide apart. Louise took the pad and tore out the page and handed the drawing back to the boy along with a large grape lollipop that seemed to appear in her hands like magic.

Turning to Flore, she said, 'The child's father should see this picture.'

Max Senior was sitting on his wooden bench on his front gallery with Jessamine when his cell phone began to ring and ring again.

'You won't believe who's on *Di Mwen*,' he kept hearing from each person who was calling him.

But he refused to turn on the radio. He didn't want to

hear it. Besides, he had never cared for that mawkish program, even when he and Louise had been on speaking terms. Out of spite – or would it be to humiliate him? – the maid in the house next door turned her radio to the loudest possible volume so that the entire neighborhood could hear.

It was hard to pretend to the lovely young woman sitting next to him that the program did not concern them, since his name was being called out nearly as often as his son's. The girl mercifully said nothing, following him into the house as he showed her his bookshelves and the abstract paintings on his living room walls, the rose garden and the swimming pool, the gazebo (the one, he realized with chagrin, that was just now being mentioned on the program). At least his cook and his gardener were not listening, he thought. Or they could be listening, like he was, catching the juicy snippets from the radio next door.

His son's friend seemed strangely unaffected. She already knew everything, he realized. Otherwise how could she not be incensed, outraged?

She was a stunning girl with an African mask of a face, all high forehead and high cheekbones, giant loop earrings, and one gold stud on either side of her cheeks. She was obviously one of those modern girls, the kind of girl whom frankly he didn't think he would be able to welcome with open arms into this family, with her cheek studs and hippie tunic and the word *POP* tattooed in red-ink calligraphy across the insides of both her wrists.

He escorted her to the kitchen, and they divided a half

pitcher of lemonade between two glasses. Surprisingly, he thought, unlike a lot of returning dyasporas, she was skinny and wasn't reeking of bug spray. He asked her why she hadn't come to the party the night before, and she said that her cousin's car had broken down and she was unable to find a ride in time. Why hadn't she called his son? he asked. She said her phone wasn't working. Couldn't she have borrowed someone else's phone? he asked. Then she confessed that she thought it was better for his son to see everyone for the first time on his own.

He wasn't sure why her explanations mattered so much to him, yet they did. He offered her some leftover codfish patties from the party. She declined. His cook was nowhere to be found and he was afraid to call out for her. He could accept neither pity nor further scorn from his employees.

He decided he wouldn't stay inside the house and hide. He would eventually have to face all of this head-on, at the school, and in any number of places in town. The girl followed him back to the porch. If the whole town wanted to parade by his open gate and condemn him, they could. He and his ex-wife had done what most parents he knew would have done. They'd tried to protect their son. And by providing the money for what had become the beauty parlor, they'd tried to protect Flore's child the best way they knew how. Should they have demanded a shotgun marriage? Should he have sent Flore off to Miami with their son? It was clear that something other than love had been made in that room that night. And perhaps that night was not the only time it had happened either. But what do you do when your misguided child, in some stupid effort to distract you from who he really is, commits a horrible act? Do you have the police come over and arrest him? Do you have him paraded on the street and humiliated on the radio? Your child. This boy. This man, who had once been a good, simple, and innocent boy. Just like this boy he had violently made. So if Flore wanted to keep this boy for herself, let her. She might have a better chance of turning him into a decent man. Good luck to her, though. He hoped she would succeed. Let her try to raise a boy and help him become a man. Let her teach him how to tie his shoes, to shake hands properly. Let her show him how to swim, how to fly a kite. Let her show him how to sharpen a blade, to shave or otherwise, how to defend himself when attacked. Let her teach him to read and write and tell him all kinds of stories, the true meaning of which he never seemed to understand. Let her feel proud, then ashamed of him, then proud again. Let her long for him when he is gone and despise him when he's in her presence. Let her wish for him to be another kind of son and for her to be another kind of mother. Let her see what it's like to protect him from even his worst desires, to keep them from tainting his life forever. Let her try to show him the difference between right and wrong. Let her guide him to adulthood unscathed in a society where people are always looking for the next person to tear down. Let her school him on legacy, how one should honor and respect it and defend it at all cost. Let her learn one day how to forgive him and eventually to forgive herself.

Flore's own mother had certainly tried to do her best for her. It must have felt like success when her daughter had landed in his house. A particular detail in Flore's story wounded him even more than the rest. The morning after the hailstorm, he had picked up his son's wet flashlight outside Flore's door and had handed it back to him.

'I forgot it there,' Junior had said. He had not questioned him further.

He had even seen Flore leave the house while he and his son were in the garden.

He had known none of the details until now, hearing what she was telling the world through the radio. He regretted not hearing anything but the storm that night. In the end, he was Max Junior's father and not hers. If he had to choose between anyone and his son, his son would always come first.

Better Louise's kind of talk, he'd thought, than others. Better that kind of shame than an even worse kind. Sleeping with the house servant was not an uncommon rite of passage for young men in houses like his. 'Droit du seigneur,' his own father had called it. Though Max Senior himself had never taken part. But wasn't even the girl expecting it? The faultiness of his logic seemed obvious now in being exposed. Could he go on Louise's show next week and use that dreadful explanation to absolve his son?

Jessamine was still respectfully silent, watching the calabash trees on the street along with him until his son pulled up in front of the house in the car he had lent him to take

Flore and the boy home. When had Flore found the time to record this monstrosity of an hour? Max Senior wondered. But now his attention was on his son. His son, his brilliant scholar son, who was now cowering inside his car, hiding from him and this girl. His son, the lover of stories as a boy. Quick, he wanted to think of a story to tell him now, a story of dangerous mistakes made by both fathers and sons. Jessamine was looking at the Jeep, at his son, her eyes dancing between them and Max Senior's face. He was now seeing her in full, carving out of her dark face another impossible grandchild for himself. Even though he was with a school full of children all day long, what did he even know of young people these days? At the school and elsewhere in town, he had seen several groups go from matènèl, prekindergarten, to close to his son's age. Not many lived out their early promise. Some of this you could blame, as his ex-wife often did, on the town, its lack of opportunities, its rigid social hierarchies. But his son, with all his opportunities and contacts, had done no better.

There was something tragic about a generation whose hopes had been raised, then dashed over and over again. Had they been poisoned by disappointment? Their leaders and elders – including himself – had made them so many promises that they'd been, for whatever reason, unable to keep. Idealists had been killed to make room for gangsters. Life had become so cheap that you could give anyone a few dollars to snuff it out. When had they entered, he wondered, what Rimbaud, in his time, had called 'le temps des assassins,' the age of assassins? Maybe his generation was the problem. They'd built a society that was useless to their children. Still, these children seemed to lack the will to sacrifice and build their own. He had been willing to at least try to make this right. He had been looking forward to turning his school over to his son, to the next generation, to see if he – they – could or would do any better. But now he might never get the chance.

He was surprised that Jessamine did not rush into his son's arms when she saw him. His son, in turn, was looking down the road, then looking back at them. Maybe the radio was on in the car and his son too was listening to the program or he was overhearing snippets from the street. Maybe he didn't even realize the program was on. Being a subject of Louise's so-called show was like getting a scarlet letter. One that at times was only temporary. You were hounded by murmurs and whispers, but only until the following week, when it was someone else's turn.

Max Senior wanted to rush to explain that to his son, to reassure him, but he hoped that Jessamine would make a move before him. Jessamine did not. Was she shell-shocked? He didn't know, but he could see in his son's face that he felt he had no choice but to quickly drive away.

Where would he go but to the beach? Aside from the lighthouse, it was his favorite place. Weighted down by more important concerns, the people at the beach might not even be listening to the show.

'Shouldn't we go after him?' the girl was asking him

now. And it seemed the kind of simple question that might be asked by someone who did not fully understand that there was nothing simple about a situation.

'Yes, we could go after him,' he replied. 'But I suspect if he wanted to be with us, he would have stayed.'

'Then what are we supposed to do?' she asked. Both of them were staring out at the front gate, at the calabash trees on the road, their branches stagnant in the heat.

'We wait,' Max Senior said, which was the usual course when it came to his son. He was always waiting for him: waiting for him to come to his senses, waiting for him to understand his duties, waiting for him to take up his responsibilities, waiting for him to return home.

'Do you think he'll come back?' asked the girl.

'He will,' Max Senior said, fully certain of this, if nothing else. 'He always does.' The girl shook her studded face and grimaced, now allowing her frustration to show. She pulled a cell phone out of her purse and dialed it. She was trying to call his son, Max Senior assumed. But hadn't she just told him that her phone wasn't working? He wanted to remind her of this, but said nothing. She held the phone up to her ear for a while and when there was no answer, she threw it back in her purse. She kept watching the front gate, the road, leaning forward as if to better see each passerby. She remained sitting there next to him, long after the show ended and the station switched to a music program, and the neighbor's maid finally lowered the volume.

'We're not going to take it sitting down,' Max Senior said,

then he realized how ridiculous that sounded because they were actually sitting down.

'I'll find Flore and Pamaxime again,' he continued, 'and I will go to the radio station myself and denounce Louise on her own airwaves.' He was rambling now, he realized. 'Nothing will change, not with the school, not with my son. All of this will be forgotten.' But what about Pamaxime? he wondered. What would become of Pamaxime?

'Byen. Okay,' the girl said.

He thought of her few words, in her heavy English accent, as banalities of the kind people say when they are feeling the opposite. He had been young once and might have said something like this, but never to one of his friends' parents. But this girl was saying this to him now, because in some way she considered herself equal to him. She might even consider herself wiser than him, her apparent lack of condemnation, her friendship with his son a sign – or so she probably thought – that she possessed a kind of compassion that surpassed everyone else's, that even surpassed his.

Just then, thankfully, his friend Albert walked through the front gate and on the path toward them. Jessamine jumped up as if she thought it was his son returning, or maybe she was just grateful to have someone else there.

'I'm not dead, am I?' Max Senior shouted to his friend.

Albert laughed, then walked faster, shifting his hat from one hand to the other when he reached them. Albert bowed his head in Jessamine's direction while tapping his hat against his thigh. Jessamine looked up at him and returned his greeting with a nod. Then, as if she could restrain herself no longer, she reached into her bag and pulled out a lighter and a cigarette. Walking to the end of the gallery, she sat on the edge of the railing and lit it. Max Senior was curious to see if smoke would come out of the side of her face through the studs in her dimples. (It didn't.) He was also horrified to see her dropping her cigarette ashes, then the cigarette butt itself, on the African violets around the porch. Some of the flowers were already withering from the increasingly hot temperatures. He had planted them around the front gallery in corners where there was neither too much light nor too much shade. He had made sure that there was the right balance of perlite and soil, and now she was using his flowers as an ashtray. He wanted to shout at her to move away from them, but before he could say anything, she started walking back toward him and his friend. She walked, he realized, as though she were doing an upright backstroke, rotating her arms with every step.

Albert was watching her too, as he had sat in her place on the bench, leaving her with no choice but either to squeeze in next to them or to remain standing. She chose to remain standing.

Had she not been there, Max Senior would have gone inside and picked up his dominoes and card table, and he and Albert would have talked nonsense and played a long game late into the night. But she was standing there looking at them, and they could not ignore her.

Max Senior could see that his friend was doing his best to

take a break now and then from staring at her face. Because of his work as an undertaker, Albert was naturally intrigued by body modifications, amputations as well as embellishments, especially rare markings or piercings. His friend had probably never seen piercings like the ones on the girl's cheeks. What would one call them, Max Senior wondered, earrings, but not on ears, zanno machwa, cheek rings? His friend, he was certain, was probably imagining his own son and daughter in the United States with these cheek rings, or worse.

'Are you here because of that program?' Max Senior asked Albert, in part to divert his friend's attention from the young lady.

'Am I only allowed to come here when you have parties?' he asked.

'You can also come when we have tragedies,' Max Senior said.

'I can't stay long,' Albert said, his eyes returning to Jessamine. She wrapped her arms around one of the porch's pillars while looking at the trees on the road.

Max Senior could imagine how much his friend would taunt him at the next marathon domino game about having a girl like this – striking, as slender as a dancer, studded, tattooed – as his daughter-in-law.

'Where is your wife?' Max Senior asked his friend.

'She's already left,' he said.

Max Senior thought how sad it had been that his friend's wife and children had not even come home for his swearing-in as mayor, because the twins were in some kind of swimming tournament. That day Max Senior had been grateful for his own divorce. How can some people not fully understand their ability to shatter hearts?

Jessamine walked back over to the far end of the porch and stared down at the same African violets she'd doubtless singed with her cigarette.

'What are these flowers?' she called out.

'Violets,' he told her.

'They grow here?' she asked.

They are growing, aren't they? he wanted to say. At least they were trying to, before your cigarette.

'Everything can grow here,' he replied instead.

Max Senior then wished that his friend had not come so soon, that it was still just him and the girl talking in this new way about things, about his son being okay and about African violets. Max Senior then realized that he hadn't properly introduced her to his friend.

'Albert, this is Jessamine,' he said. 'Remember, we were waiting for her last night. Jessamine, this is Albert Vincent, an old friend.'

'Old only in the length of my friendship with Max,' Albert said.

'I see.' The girl did smile this time.

'And where is Junior now?' Albert asked.

Max Senior shrugged. 'Most likely at the beach. Or at the lighthouse,' he added.

'Let him be,' Albert advised. 'He'll come back when he's ready. Let's just let him be.'

'That's what I told Jessamine here,' Max Senior said.

It was getting dark, and Max Senior's hope that his son would return grew stronger. Otherwise, it would be up to him to decide where to put the girl for the night. She had somehow reached his house on a camion that her relatives had put her in from the capital. The driver had been kind enough to drop her off at the gate, but she had no sure way of going back to Port-au-Prince, at least not tonight.

'I suppose you heard the program,' Max Senior said, keeping his eyes on the few people walking by on the road, looking, he thought, with new interest at his house.

'Part of it,' Albert said, resting his head on the wall behind him. 'I heard it after meeting with the mother of a young man who got a machete in his gut from a land dispute, so I had some perspective.'

Jessamine raised an eyebrow, looking curious in a way that seemed to flatter his friend.

'You're Oncle Albert,' she said. 'Maxime told me about you.'

'Did he?' Albert said. 'I thought he had forgotten about all of us.'

'Seems like no one here forgot him, though,' the girl said.

'Did he want us to forget him?' Max Senior asked, ashamed when he heard how forlorn his own voice sounded.

'Of course, as Louise constantly reminds us, there are things we should never forget,' Albert said, as though lecturing his friend.

'Kolangèt manman Louise, screw her!' Max Senior shouted, finally allowing himself to blurt out the full extent of his anger: at himself, at his son, at Flore, but most especially at Louise George.

Jessamine shrank back a little, hugging the porch pillar tighter, as if to give him room. Looking at her face, her high brow, her tattoo, and her pierced cheeks, Max could sense some deeper story there, some story he would probably never know. Albert said nothing, letting his friend stew for a moment. Instead he placed his hat on his lap, allowing his hands to shake openly for her to see.

It was growing even darker now, so dark that on Max Senior's street one could already see lights through the windows of a few houses. The silence among the three of them now bothered Max Senior so much that he did not feel as timid as he might have asking what he did next.

'Are you and my son in love?' he asked. 'Nou renmen?'

Once the words crossed his lips, he realized that they sounded more like a plea than a question. Please, please, love my son was really what he was saying. And for once he was grateful that Albert restrained himself from jumping in and facetiously asking, for example, 'Who, me? Am I in love with your son?' Instead it was the girl who asked, 'Me?' and Max Senior said, 'Since we're neither on the radio nor on television, I'm going to both nod and say yes.'

Max Senior nodded and Jessamine frowned her disapproval at his poking fun at the show and at Flore.

'Your son is my friend,' she said, her eyes following the

fireflies lighting up, then disappearing around them. 'He is my very terrible and imperfect and dear friend.'

Max Senior thought this an accurate description, one of many he might have used himself.

'I fell in love with your son when I met him and knew nothing about him,' she continued.

'And he?' Max Senior interrupted her to ask. 'Did he fall in love with you?'

'What do you think?' she asked brazenly.

'Obviously he doesn't know what to think,' Albert interjected. 'That's why he's asking you.'

'As lovable as I am,' she said, now waving her hands as though to reach for the fireflies, 'he is not capable of being in love with me.'

'How's that?' asked Max Senior.

'I thought you would already know this,' the girl said to Max Senior as plainly as she had said everything else. 'Your son has been in love only once in his life, and the person he was in love with is dead.'

Max Junior was lying on his back, under the palms that inclined as though to touch the sea. He tucked his hands under his head and stared up at the dark clouds, which were blocking, then fleeing the moon. That everyone could and should despise him, there was no question, and they had good reason. Flore most of all.

He remembered the hailstorm that seemed like it might

pummel the world to pieces. He remembered her flailing arms. He had foolishly wanted to prove something to his father that night, that he could be with Flore. He wanted his father to hear her screams.

To this day, he had never been with any man but Bernard. He and Bernard would come to the beach on nights like this and would remove their shirts, then plunge into the water. Initially, Bernard had been afraid of the sea. He was a strong swimmer, but was always worried that he would be caught in a current and towed away. That he would disappear forever.

Now, as he walked fully clothed to the water, Max Junior thought of his father's version of a Cornish folktale, one the old man had told him when he was little.

A boy is lured into the woods by music. The deeper the boy walks into the woods, the denser the woods become and the more beautiful the music. The boy follows this music until he gets so lost that he no longer knows where he is. He becomes so scared that he wants to return home, but he also wants to follow the music to see where it leads. After he walks so far that the woods become impassable, he begins to cry for help. And that's when a spirit emerges and makes a path for him. The path leads to the sea, where suddenly the music stops and the boy is now so tired that he lies down and falls asleep. When he wakes up, the boy finds himself back home, safely in his own bed, with his head full of music and mermaids and crystal palaces under the sea. The spirit in the woods saved this boy, his father said, because the spirit wanted the boy to remain innocent and good and that innocence and goodness was as precious as the dreams she'd placed in his head. And because of that innocence and goodness, she would watch over him forever.

Max Junior now slipped into the water, feeling the cool waves rise and fall around him as the water ballooned his red shirt, the one Jessamine had given him for his return trip home. In the sea, he thought of music, the rap-filled kind he had once played on his radio show, the kind Bernard had liked. He also thought of flowers and birds. He thought of the birdhouses he and his father had built together, after hours of schoolwork and judo practice, when he was a boy. He thought of the somber plumage of some petrels and storm-signaling seagulls. He thought of the pigeons, alive and dead, in Bernard's stories. He thought of the orchids and roses in his father's garden, the dragonflies that buzzed around after a heavy rain and the fireflies that bombarded them at night. He thought of how the roses had been pummeled the night of the hailstorm but had still had enough nectar to attract a hummingbird the next morning. He thought of yellow jasmine, his mother's favorite flowers. She would tie a bouquet to the bell on the front of her bicycle, then the two of them would ride next to each other through town. They would ride to the kleren factory and his mother, sniffing the air, would become giddy from the raw liquor smell. He thought of his mother's history lessons about the ruins of Abitasyon Pauline. He remembered the talk they'd had in the middle of the ruins shortly before she left town. You are who you love, she'd told him. You try to mend what you've torn. But remember that love is like kerosene. The more you have, the more you burn.

He liked his mother's blunt aphorisms. He also liked how she tried to explain the rogue waves. Lasirèn, she said, made her presence known by swelling a wave several feet, whenever she craved human company.

One night ten years ago, after he'd learned that Flore was pregnant, he was sitting alone on the gallery of the old Anthère lighthouse when he thought he saw a supernova exploding above the sea. It was so dazzling that he could make out the uneven edges and emission line, even after closing his eyes. That's when he also thought he saw the night sea swirl into a massive funnel, as if a mid-ocean whirlpool had come near the shore. Then the same waters quietly retreated – a tsunami in reverse – the waves turning into liquid mountains. He stood up, pressing his ribs into the lighthouse railing until he saw what he believed was part of the seafloor, a mountain-size ridge with reefs and sandbanks stripped bare for miles. Then just as quickly, the waves buckled and the water collapsed, hastily covering the ocean floor, as if nothing had taken place.

He had wondered then whether he was in shock, or overtired, or hallucinating. But now he believed that he had neither dreamed nor imagined all this, that it had actually happened.

He was remembering this, he knew, as a way of avoiding thinking about his son. He imagined the *0* face drawing melting, coming apart, even now in his pants pocket. A drawing made by his son, whom he'd just met, his son, whom he might never see again. Would meeting him today have meant anything at all to his son? How long would it take the boy to forget him? Would his son grow up calling another man 'Papa'? And if he did, would there ever be some hesitation, a hint of doubt in the back of the boy's mind, something that would ring false in the sound of his voice? The worst possible case of unrequited love, Jessamine had told him, was feeling rejected by a parent. Was the second worst being rejected by your child? He knew quite a bit about unrequited love, unreciprocated love. Until he'd met his son, he'd felt as if every other love were a phantom version, a shadow of the one he'd once had.

People like to say of the sea that lanmè pa kenbe kras, the sea does not hide dirt. It does not keep secrets. The sea was both hostile and docile, the ultimate trickster. It was as large as it was small, as long as you could claim a portion of it for yourself. You could scatter both ashes and flowers in it. You could take as much as you wanted from it. But it too could take back. You could make love in it and you could surrender to it, and oddly enough, surrendering at sea felt somewhat like surrendering on land, taking a deep breath and simply letting go. You could just as easily lie down in the sea as you might in the woods, and simply fall asleep.

*

Nozias's eyes had been closed for only a few minutes when he was awakened by a strange sound in the water, echoes of a person crying. Or was it laughter?

He felt a chill, shuddering as he made his way to the edge of the water. A few of his friends, the other fishermen who'd left their own shacks to surround him in support, were still fast asleep, their bodies strewn in fetal positions around him on the sand. Others, he knew, were in town or up by the lighthouse, looking for his daughter.

Was it Claire Limyè Lanmè he had just heard in this water, though? he wondered. Was that what had awakened him, the draft of her spirit drifting past, the gust of her final breaths? He'd felt something similar the day his wife died. It was hard to explain, but in his wife's case, it was a momentary stillness, as though the entire world had grown completely silent.

He was feeling this now, but not as strongly. Could it be Claire sinking in? Or Caleb settling at the bottom of the sea?

He peered out into the water, and the seaweed mixed with the reflection of the night sky made it seem as though there were stardust on its surface. He squeezed his arms around his body as if to hold himself in one piece while he waited for the girl's voice to surface from the waves.

'Papa, se ou?'

Some mornings when he would walk into their shack from the sea, Claire would ask in a half-sleeping voice, 'Papa, is that you?'

'Ki yès ankò?' he would ask. 'Who else would it be?'

Now, he hurried back to the shack, remembering midstep that he'd left Madame Gaëlle there. And when he walked in, the lamp was still burning.

Madame Gaëlle and her shiny dress hadn't moved from the edge of his bed. She was watching the lamp wick's shadows flicker across the newspaper-covered walls when he cried out, 'Daughter, was that you?'

The midwife had told him that his wife's last words before she died had been to Claire's crowning head and shoulders. Though feeble and weak, she had still managed to say, 'Vini.' Come. But she was gone before Claire came.

He closed the door and pressed his back against it, again not knowing what to say.

'Did you find her?' Madame Gaëlle asked.

He shook his head no.

The day before Claire Limyè Lanmè's seventh birthday, he had gone to his friend Caleb to request a special favor. Caleb was one of a handful of his fisherman friends who could read and write, so Caleb acted as his and some of the other fishermen's document checker and letter writer. The fact that Caleb's wife was a deaf mute – she was always present during his letter writing – also guaranteed that the words dictated in her presence would not spread through the town's teledyòl gossip mill.

Nozias had gone to Caleb to have him look over the documents that would be required should Madame Gaëlle adopt Claire. There was Claire's birth certificate and school report cards, which showed her to be excelling at everything, including good behavior. But sitting in Caleb's shack, which was twice as big as his, he decided at the very last minute to dictate a letter to Claire.

At sixty-nine, Caleb was older than most of the men who were still going out on the water. Unlike most of the fishermen, whose hands looked as though they had been sliced many times over and patched back together, Caleb's hands were the smoothest, and the smallest, that Nozias had ever seen on a grown man. The way Caleb copied the words that spilled out of his mouth seemed magical to him. Nozias was astonished when Caleb read his words back to him. The phrases, as few and as banal as they were, seemed gentler, neater, as if Caleb had entered his head and reorganized everything.

Madame Gaëlle now watched as he walked to his cot and raised the pillow where his head usually lay. They were close enough that she could reach over and touch the back of his smooth, bald head with her hands. He pulled out the black plastic bag in which Claire Limyè Lanmè's papers and his letter were carefully wrapped. He untied the bag, taking special care not to tear any holes in it. He pulled out the letter and handed it to her.

Madame Gaëlle squinted as though she were having trouble seeing the words, then she slid down to be closer to the lamp, leaving even less space between them.

She began reading the letter to herself, then raised her voice:

Claire Limyè Lanmè,

I thank God for the ability to use my voice to dictate this letter to you. Claire, please remember these things I am about to tell you. No matter what you might hear later in your life, I am not doing this for money. I did not sell you. I am giving you a better life. Please be nice to Madame and do everything she tells you. Continue to do well in school and you will grow up to be a smart and important woman. Also remember to not sleep on your back, so you won't have bad dreams. And don't ever forget your papa because I will never forget you. That is all I wish to say for now. Thank you for taking the time to read these words.

Nozias Faustin, Your Father

Madame Gaëlle refolded the letter and returned it to the bag. She pressed her lips against the back of his neck, letting them linger there in a kiss.

He hadn't been kissed by a woman in that way since his wife died, a kiss so pure that it felt like it was polishing him. He felt as though his body had turned to gold. A stream of light was coursing through him, and when he reached up to touch her face, he felt both their bodies expand beyond the size of his room.

'What will we do when Claire returns?' she asked, removing her lips from the back of his neck, sliding, slipping away from his side of the cot, away from him. Yet she had said 'nou,' we, and he was glad that she had said it.

What will *we* do when Claire returns?

This is what he wanted more than anything for his daughter: a lack of cruelty, a feeling of safety, but also love. Benevolence and sympathy too, but mostly love.

He wasn't sure what he would do when Claire returned. He didn't know. Maybe he would still have Claire go live with her. Or maybe he would postpone again for another year. Then another. Then another. And soon he would see for himself whether what people said about children growing up so fast was true for more than seven years. Avan w bat zye w. In the flicker of an eyelid. Before you know it, they're living their own lives. Maybe Claire would be old enough by then to be the one leaving him behind. Or maybe something terrible would happen to him before she was grown. Or maybe, like Caleb, he would be lost at sea and Madame Gaëlle would remember that tonight a promise had been extracted from her. She had said yes. She had said 'nou.' She had agreed to take Claire. But first Claire had to come back. And when she did, would she come back to live with him? Would they have another year together, on the beach? This is what he hoped his wife might have said, if she'd found herself in his position, giving their child away: better a child cry for a parent now then for everything later on. But would she, could she – she his wife, she his daughter, and she Madame Gaëlle – could they even see it like that?

Madame Gaëlle got up and moved to Claire's cot so that she was now across from him, facing him.

'I want to ask you again,' she said, 'why you want to give her away. And to me.'

'I am not the first,' he said, trying to remain calm, to stay composed, 'nor am I the only one to ever give up a child.'

'I used to see you,' she said, 'walking by the fabric store, on your way to visit her at the funeral parlor. You loved that woman, her mother, so much . . .'

And with those words still in the air, Nozias abruptly got up and walked out of the shack once again, hoping to avoid this part of the exchange, to avoid thinking how much even the idea of giving away their daughter would have devastated his wife. And what if both Claires were now gone for good? What if he never saw his daughter again?

After he'd stepped outside, Gaëlle thought she heard him scream. She grabbed the kerosene lamp and rushed out the door, and to the sea, to the edge of the water, where he was standing with the waves lapping at his feet.

Nozias Faustin had indeed loved his wife. And one way he liked to show it was by visiting her at the funeral parlor where she worked, whenever he wasn't out at sea. One afternoon when he got to the funeral parlor, she was scrubbing the waist-high cement table where she washed and dressed the dead. The table was attached to the floor and was wide enough for two or three people to be laid out comfortably. But only his wife was there when he arrived.

During his visits, he would often find her in the middle of her work, her small frame swimming in her sand-colored plastic work coat, her long, gloved fingers wiping beads of water off a naked corpse. Sometimes it was someone he recognized and he would wonder how she could touch so intimately in death someone she had spoken to in life. Sometimes, if they had drowned, the bodies would be bloated, unrecognizable. On those occasions, she would hand him a cloth mouth-and-nose cover, just like hers, and would then seem to forget that he was there. She would talk to the dead instead. Moving her masked face close to their ears, she would recount everything that had happened in town since they had died.

Most of the time, she would, he knew, have other company than him. Family members would come and help wash and dress. She would tell him later that she had watched them for hints of tenderness that she'd then apply to those whose family members preferred not to come. Sometimes she would apply special perfumes, sneak in a pair of socks or stockings of her own choosing, though the dead were never to have shoes. Shoes could only weigh a person down in the afterlife.

She would sew some of the clothes for the dead, especially the babies, for whom it was too heartbreaking to buy burial clothes, but whenever necessary, she would adjust the clothes that were brought in, which were often either too large or too small. She would also tell him about families who would bury the dead in a secret place, ahead of the cement-filled closed coffin at the funeral service, for fear that their dead might be snatched from the cemetery and turned into zombies. She often marveled how so many of the photographs brought in for the funeral programs were from decades ago; a centenarian's funeral program cover photo was usually a wedding portrait or a special-occasion likeness from when the person was barely out of adolescence.

Every now and then, she would be asked by the family to extract gold crowns from the dead's mouth, but that she would never dare to do herself. She would ask Msye Albert to do that.

She was glad, she sometimes told Nozias, that she never had to go into the walk-in freezer to take a corpse off the shelf by herself, not even a baby corpse, which she could have easily lifted and carried. Whenever she had to wash and dress the bodies, she would find them already on the table waiting.

Nozias was there once when she was putting a final dab of powder on a young man's face, and both the man's eyes abruptly popped open. Nozias had jumped back, terrified, but she hadn't even flinched.

'I just have to tell Msye Albert to sele, or set, the eyes again,' she said as she went on with her work.

Setting the eyes, he learned that day, did not mean placing one's fingers over the eyelids and sliding them downward, as he had seen laypeople do. Rather, it meant putting thumbprint-size pieces of rubber under the eyelids, then gluing them to the insides of the eyes so they would remain closed.

Some of the corpses would break wind as if they were alive, except it was a fouler, stinkier wind. But there was no such smell that day, just the lingering fragrance of the lemon-scented disinfectant she scrubbed the cement table with after she washed each body.

As he walked toward her in the washroom that afternoon, she did not rush to greet him. The plastic coat she was wearing was weighing her down, he thought, or maybe it was something else.

He could hear above him, around him, the creaking and echoes coming from other parts of the house, the loud footsteps and muffled conversations from the offices upstairs. Next to the room they were in was the showroom, with the sample coffins lined against the wall. Next to that was the chapel with a stained-glass window of the Last Supper, made locally, with brown faces, by a Ville Rose artist.

His wife removed her work coat, letting it fall at her feet. Underneath she was wearing her favorite dress, a bell-shaped parrot-green dress that she had sewn herself. Her hair was neatly brushed, the cornrows lined up like roads on a map to some mysterious land. Her hands were folded over her breasts and she closed her eyes, looking as though she were sleeping on her feet. He wondered if this was what she'd been doing before he'd come in, listening with her eyes closed to everything around her.

'We are no longer two. Now we are three,' she said. He

opened his eyes wide. Her childlike face, her usually serene childlike face, was tied in an inexplicable knot as though she were fighting back tears.

'How do you tell someone you're pregnant in a funeral parlor?' he asked when she was done speaking. He was too delighted not to laugh. He rushed over and grabbed her, then stepped back for fear of crushing her. She was laughing too when he threw his arms around her. Then he was a bit sad, and his sadness, mingled with intense joy, made him hold her tight again. How does life itself, as much as you must want it in your body, not feel futile when you have seen so many dead?

She'd told him about pregnant mothers that she'd dressed for their burial with the babies still inside them. How could this not have been on her mind that afternoon?

'I told Msye Albert,' she said, 'that I won't be washing and dressing the dead anymore.'

He had grown used to the dead being part of her life. Because she had touched so many corpses, some of their friends and neighbors wouldn't even allow her to shake their hands or wouldn't eat the food she cooked. But he was happy to live with all of that, if it meant living with her. Sometimes he could even smell the dead on her, in the embalming fluids and disinfectant. The hands that stroked the faces of the dead stroked his. He ate from those hands. He kissed them. He loved them. He loved their constellations of scars from all the sewing she did without thimbles. He loved how rough her fingertips could feel, how like a tiny grater, even when she was gentle. And he knew that her sympathy for the dead, her compassion for everyone, would make her a good mother, a great mother.

That afternoon in the funeral parlor, it was as if life had sprung up to embrace him, even in this place of death. He raised her dress to her waist, bent down and pressed his ear against her still-flat stomach and held it there, listening for some faint new sounds.

'I told the baby not to tell you anything yet,' she joked.

After she died, he would remember seeing her body laid out on the cot where they had slept together since she had come to live with him. He was shocked to see that, in death, though the baby was no longer in it, her stomach was still round like a frigate bird's bill.

The midwife had put that same parrot-green dress on his wife and it looked small, too tight on her body. Her dead hands were folded over her chest in a way that had reminded him of how she'd been standing against the wall in the funeral parlor the afternoon he'd learned that she was pregnant. When he bent over and pressed his ear against her belly in the wash-and-dress room, she kept muttering, 'Sa se pa nou. Se pa nou. This is ours. Ours. Ours. Ours.'

Claire de Lune

SOMETIMES CLAIRE LIMYÈ LANMÈ FAUSTIN would dream about the day she was born. In her dream, it was a gray morning and the sky too was pregnant, with rain. On one side of the room was a brand-new sisal broom, which, as in many home births, a midwife would brush across her mother's bare stomach to help 'sweep' her out. On the other side of the room would be a chair with a yellow baby sheet draped over it. A breeze would flow under the sheet, making it rise and fall along with her mother's breath. The echo of the heart that had been thumping so loudly above her head would stop as two hands would free her shoulders, then yank her out.

'A revenan,' she would hear the midwife saying. 'She is a revenan.'

This would mean, of course, that her mother had died.

Soon after she was born, the midwife would wash her body, plunging her into a pot of blood-warm water, then the midwife would use the same water to wash her mother. In the dream, Claire would glimpse her mother as the midwife raised her out of the water. Her mother is bony and long and laid out on her father's cot in a leaf-colored dress. Her mother's face is turned sideways, showing the highest peak of a cheekbone. Over her mother appears her father's face and the furrows of concern carved into it, like miniatures graves.

Then she would dream of breasts, full, cushiony, pillow-like breasts, whose tips would turn from flesh to rubber, and she would dream of her feet becoming dusty when she walked on the ground, and of rivers becoming muddy when she stepped into them, and she would wake up wishing that she could stay asleep forever, just so that she could see more of these things in her dreams and fully understand them. And finally she might understand why in her real, waking life she had to wash herself in buckets beside the latrines behind the shacks when there was water everywhere, although it was seawater and if you bathed in seawater, you would get a layer of salt on your skin that looked like ash and dust and when you put your tongue on your arm you would taste salt like you tasted salt when you secretly ran your tongue over your father's gutted and salted fish and your tongue would bleed from rubbing against the salted scales and the salt would sting where you had cut your tongue, making the salt even more delicious.

Salt was life, she would often hear the adults say. Some of the fishermen's wives would throw a pinch of crushed salt in the air for good luck, before their men left for the sea. (Some would also refuse to eat, or wash, or comb their hair until their men came back.) When zombies ate salt, it brought them back to life. Or so she'd always heard. Maybe if she ate enough salt, she would finally understand why her father wouldn't let her wander, flannen. She would always try, though. Sometimes while her father was at sea, she would walk through the open market and pretend that she was one of those children sent to buy provisions to bring home to a mother. And she would pick up things at the market and put them down, raising, then crushing the hopes of the vendors, who would mumble under their breath as she walked away.

Every now and again one of the vendors would shout, 'Just like her mother!' and she would ask herself what else she might do to make them say even more often that she was just like her mother. Besides dying, that is.

Aside from hearing the vendors say that she was just like her mother, she liked walking through the market because everything there was mixed in, the braying goats, the cackling chickens, the vegetables in season, her favorite of which was breadfruit, because people called breadfruit lam veritab, veritable souls. She would have liked to have flannen into the seaside eating places and hotels too, the ones where the women were said to spend days and nights in their bras and panties and the men walked in the doors quickly as if they were too frightened of being seen. But these places were not for children, and she'd heard her father say, when he'd been told that she'd wandered too far off course and had approached one of those places, that a girl who went into a place like that might not come out the same. She might enter a girl and someone might put a hand over her mouth and she might come out bleeding between her legs and people would start calling her Madame, because she would no longer be considered a girl. If she went anywhere near those places, her father had told her, people would whisper behind her back that she was the Madame of many men. There had been a girl in school like that, who'd had someone put his hands over her mouth, someone who had made her bleed between her legs. The girl had to leave school after that. People in town talked about the schoolmaster's son like that too. They called him a Madame, another kind of Madame, they said. They also said that he had stolen (vòlè) or he had violated (vyole) a girl who had (vole) flown away. Vòlè vyole w, ou vole. The girl who had vole, flown away, wasn't a girl anymore but a woman, a woman who later had a child by the schoolmaster's son. It was like one of those stories Madame Louise George used to read to the preschool matènèl classes when Madame Louise was still coming to the school. In Madame Louise's stories, everything was organized a certain way; everything was neat. Things would start out well, but would end up being bad, then would be well again. Claire didn't believe stories like that, even when she felt like they were aimed at her, even when they were meant to defend her or teach her some kind of lesson. She disliked people too sometimes. She felt them moving around her, exchanging places. Sometimes she wished people, especially adults, were trees. If only trees could move. With trees, you'd have to be the one who moved around them. But trees didn't cry. They didn't complain.

People liked to complain. Even her father, who was usually so quiet. Yet most people thought they were smarter than trees because they could talk. But talking wasn't everything. Who cared if you could talk, if you decided to get up and leave? That was why the smartest person she knew was Madame Josephine.

Madame Josephine had no voice, so she made up a new language with her hands. It was a more direct language than the one the other adults spoke. Her father knew this hand language, and people could understand Madame Josephine because of him. It was as if her father and Madame Josephine could have been twins, born at the same hour on the same day. She wondered what people would have said if she and her mother had died on the same day. For a while they were twinned, when she was inside her mother's body. But she never dreamed of being inside her mother's body, except in that last moment when she had to come out and that last moment always made her think of water.

Sometimes when she was lying on her back in the sea, her toes pointed, her hands facing down, her ears half submerged, while she was listening to both the world above and beneath the water, she yearned for the warm salty water to be her mother's body, the waves her mother's heartbeat, the sunlight the tunnel that guided her out the day her mother died. From the sea, even while lying on her back, she could see her home on the beach and above it the houses on the hill and the Anthère lighthouse and above that all the densely packed ferns of Mòn Initil. At night, it was impossible to see

Mòn Initil. Even when a full moon was parked right above it and it attracted dozens of shooting stars, Mòn Initil still looked like a blank spot at the foot of the sky. This was just as well, because people were afraid of Mòn Initil.

One story that Madame Louise had read to the class when Claire was smaller said that people were afraid to go to Mòn Initil because that's where in the olden days the slaves who had escaped the old Abitasyon Pauline had gone to hide, and some of them had never made it out. The bones of our ancestors, Madame Louise had said in her croaky voice, still litter the grounds of Mòn Initil, and their ghosts still haunt its trees.

In the daytime, though, and from the water, Mòn Initil looked harmless, even inviting. The ground was naturally terraced so the trees were neatly lined up in rows, each one taller than the last. The Anthère lighthouse was ugly in the daytime, and sometimes, with the sun shining overhead, it was all rocks sticking out of cement when it did not look washed out altogether. But at night, especially nights when someone was missing or dead, it was lit up like a super moon. And it glowed.

She had never been up to the top of the Anthère lighthouse, in the gallery, but she imagined that if ever she were to go, it would be to say good-bye to her father if he were lost at sea. It would be to light a lamp or swing a flashlight one night, hoping that he would see it from the water.

'A few moments earlier and it would have been me,' her father had told her that very morning. And what would she have done if it had been him? Where would she have gone if the fabric vendor had said no yet again? Who would have taken her in for the rest of her life? There were the relatives in the mountain village, her mother's people, who showed up at Christmas sometimes with yams and bread-fruit, which they knew she liked. But aside from that, she never saw them. They would appear again and she would have to follow them up to the mountain and she would have to leave her school and the one or two children in her class who spoke to her. But would she see her father again? He was giving her away to the fabric vendor, the woman whose breasts were the first she had suckled, as he liked to remind everyone. Why hadn't he just given her to this woman after she had suckled her breasts? she wondered. She would have known no other life. She would have used her first word to call this woman 'Manman.' She would have cried for her when she was sick. She would have pouted at her when she was scolded. She would have held her hand on the way to and from school. She would have known the woman's dead child as her sister and she would have had a sister to mourn, rather than a mother. It might have been all the same. She would not have remembered much about the sister either. All she would know would be the empty space that this sister would have occupied, without being able to define it. She had no idea what it was to have a mother rather than a string of motherly acts performed by different hands: the aunt in the mountains – who'd had her the first three years of her life, the neighbors, including Madame Josephine, who'd motion for her to come out of the sea when she'd been in there too long. Her father often took her to the cemetery to visit her mother, but if it had been up to her, if she had had a say, they would have been visiting her mother at sea, because her mother would have been buried at sea. It was clear that her mother had liked the sea. Both her mother and father must have loved the sea to have given her that name. If only he spoke more, her father. If only he would share with her the pieces of her mother he had enjoyed. If only those pieces of her mother could be placed in a box for her to open every day. One moment would suffice, one important moment that involved more than the word 'Vini' that she'd heard him tell people about.

'It was my wife's last word and it was to Claire,' he liked to say. 'And yet by the time Claire came her mother was already gone.'

The way he told the story always made her feel like someone who had shown up uninvited somewhere, as if she shouldn't have come. As if her mother's death were her fault. Other times he seemed so happy that she was here. She could sometimes see him watching her while she was doing her homework. He would pretend he was repairing a net or sharpening a stick into a toothpick while sitting on his cot across the room, but he would be watching her, as though he were looking for something, something he could never find. Maybe he was looking for her mother. The women who combed her hair, the vendors whose products she picked up and laid down, all said that she looked like her mother. 'Like two drops of water,' they said. She must walk like her mother too, and when she was a woman, a true Madame, when her adult voice came in, would she sound like her mother too? Or would she continue to confuse with her presence the people who had known her mother? Maybe they would take her for her mother, when her body was filled in, when her chest had fully grown, when she became a woman.

Now she would have a mother, but not a mother whom she looked like. Only for one moment, for one word ('Vini'), had she had the mother she looked like anyway.

While playing wonn, when she held hands with other girls, either at school or on the beach, when they swayed their arms up and down before taking off in their circle, when they were deciding which way to play or which song to sing, she would always think of the same song. Sometimes she suggested it and it was shouted down, and other times she kept it to herself, and whatever the other girls were singing, she would sing that one particular song in her head. She even sang it when she jumped rope, when no one was singing anything. And whenever she sang it, it was as if someone else were there with her. When there were five other girls playing, if she moved faster than anyone else, she would see seven shadows on the ground.

> Lasirèn, Labalèn
> Chapo m tonbe nan lanmè
> Lasirèn, The Whale
> My hat fell into the sea

The other girls didn't always like this song because it was not a real wonn song. It was a fisherman's song. Although the melody was cheerful, the words were sad. You never got back things that fell into the sea. She was surprised that the granmoun, the adults, were not singing this song all day long. So much had fallen into the sea. Hats fell into the sea. Hearts fell into the sea. So much had fallen into the sea. So much could still fall into the sea, including Msye Caleb, who fell in that morning, and all the men like her father who went there to look for fish. She was always afraid that one day she might have to sing that song every moment of every day. Not about a hat, but about her heart, about her father. And this is why she sometimes wished the sea would disappear. If the sea disappeared, she would miss its ever-changing sounds: how it sometimes sounded like one long breath. And sometimes like a cry. She would miss thunderclaps and how the lightning that came with them momentarily brightened the farthest-out reaches of the sea. She would also miss the sea's colors: the turquoise in the distance and its light-blue ripples up close, the white foam at the peaks of the waves. She would miss the surge of high tide and the retreat of low tide, the milky or rosy clouds of dawn and the orange mists of sunsets. She would miss driftwood, sea glass, seashells, especially the baby ears and buttercups. She would miss throwing stones into the sea and seeing how far they would go. She would even miss the slimy seaweed that the sea spewed out, more during the warmer months of the year. She would also miss smelling the sea, which sometimes reminded her of wet hair. Sure, if the sea disappeared, there might be no fish to eat and she might not be able to lie on her back in it and look up at the hills from the water and sometimes see the magic of how it could be raining up in the hills and be perfectly sunny where she was. But maybe if the sea disappeared her father wouldn't have to go there anymore, and the crazy waves might not get him like they got Msye Caleb. There were more seas elsewhere, and if he left her, he might go to these other seas. They might be even stronger, crazier, more powerful seas than the one outside her front door. But in those other places he might have a bigger boat, one that was big enough for the two of them to live in, and she might be able to go with him wherever he was going and there they would live together where the crazy waves would not get them. And maybe if she sang this song all the time it would keep bad things from happening and it would keep her father from leaving, and if he stayed, from dying in this sea. But during those times when she went in and lay on her back, her face aimed at the sky, while he was in another part of this sea, someplace where she could not spot his boat, she hoped that if the sea disappeared at that moment, she would disappear with it too, and she wouldn't have to miss him and he wouldn't have to be sad and she wouldn't have to wonder all the time where he was chèche lavi, looking for a better life. But what if there was no better life? How could he not know this? How could granmoun, grown people, not understand such things? How could they not understand everything?

She had somehow tonight convinced the other girls to sing the Lasirèn song for the wonn. It was her birthday, she had told them. She was seven, she had told them. The oldest girl let her pick the song. They'd groaned when she said it, but they knew it was coming and they were prepared, and as the adults gathered around to mourn Msye Caleb, she and her friends sang that song until they were hoarse, circling until they were dizzy. And though she wanted to stop after a while, she did not want them to stop and not begin again with the same song, so she tried to hang on. It was the best seventh-birthday gift they could give her.

When Madame Gaëlle arrived, Claire somehow knew that she'd interrupt their game. And sure enough, as soon as they saw Madame Gaëlle, the other girls stopped circling and took the opportunity to escape from Claire and her song.

She could tell by the look on Madame Gaëlle's face that she had something in mind. Madame Gaëlle wanted something from her. And the only thing she had that Madame Gaëlle might want was her. It was also what her father wanted, for Madame Gaëlle to have her. At first, she was frightened by Madame Gaëlle's approach, at the careful way she moved in her direction. It was unusual too for a lady like Madame Gaëlle to be out in a fancy party gown with her hair rollers and with slippers on her feet. Something about Madame Gaëlle's mission must be pressing. At first Madame Gaëlle seemed to creep up on her, then she hovered over her, as though she were building up enough courage to ask a simple question that other adults often asked her, 'Is your papa here?'

She had to look up into Madame Gaëlle's face to answer. She didn't want to, but she had to because of the sounds of the waves and all the people visiting Madame Josephine, and whenever she was nervous her voice wasn't so loud anyway, so Madame Gaëlle wouldn't be able to understand her unless she was looking straight into Madame Gaëlle's eyes.

She wished she could explain to Madame Gaëlle before answering that she was not trying to be disrespectful by looking into her eyes. She knew that looking into an adult's eyes was as disrespectful as whistling in public or making ugly remarks about someone's mother. So instead of speaking, she nodded her answer.

Madame Gaëlle walked away, over to a big rock, then motioned for her to come and sit on another rock, next to her. She looked past Madame Gaëlle, wishing that her father could see them from wherever he was. She had not seen him for some time, but seeing her and Madame Gaëlle together would bring him running over for sure.

Before starting the wonn, she had hidden her sandals near the rock where Madame Gaëlle was now sitting. Maybe this was some sign. Maybe her sandals had chosen Madame Gaëlle. Her father would certainly see it as some kind of sign if she told him that Madame Gaëlle had come to sit where she had hidden her sandals. Maybe she should be saying something now. But she didn't know what to say and Madame Gaëlle didn't seem to know what to say either, because Madame Gaëlle didn't talk for a long time, but Claire could feel that Madame Gaëlle was watching her the way her father watched her. She took her time slipping on her sandals, not knowing how to make Madame Gaëlle's staring and not-talking stop. Then she heard Madame Gaëlle say, 'I knew your mother.'

Of course Madame Gaëlle had known her mother. Everyone in town, it seemed, had known her mother. Everyone, except her. She knew this the way she knew everything else, by hearing bits of things adults said to one another when they didn't think she was listening. Besides, her mother and Madame Gaëlle's daughter were buried together in the same part of the town cemetery where she had gone that very morning.

But wait. Was Madame Gaëlle going to tell her something about her mother that she'd never heard before, that extra thing she often wished her father would tell her? Had Madame Gaëlle wrapped a piece of her mother, an invisible piece, in an invisible box, that she now wanted to open for her to visit? Were her mother and Madame Gaëlle friends? Is that why Madame Gaëlle had nursed her that one time, making Madame Gaëlle, as her father liked to say, her milk mother? She wanted to hear more. What could she do to hear more? She raised her head and looked directly into Madame Gaëlle's eyes. It was not disrespectful if it was urgent, if you wanted something and couldn't ask. It was not disrespect. It was curiosity. It was like Madame Josephine, who, because she could not speak, had to look in the faces of all people, even the white doctors at Sainte Thérèse when they were trying to talk to her about her leg. But white people didn't care if you looked into their eyes – that's what the people who'd seen them up close at L'hôpital Sainte Thérèse said. The white people there actually wanted you to look into their eyes. That's how they claimed to know you were being honest. So she was now looking into Madame Gaëlle's wild, mournful eyes and she was pretending that Madame Gaëlle was one of those white people who didn't care if you looked into their eyes, even as a stream of words came pouring out of Madame Gaëlle's mouth.

'Your mother had sewn so many things for you,' Madame Gaëlle was saying, but in a jumble, as if to herself. 'She had sewn little dresses for you even before she was pregnant with you.' Then Madame Gaëlle said something about God. No, not God, God's hands. Her mother, Madame Gaëlle said, had stolen her from God's hands. 'And then you were born,' Madame Gaëlle said, her voice clear now. And the revenan talk, Madame Gaëlle was saying she didn't believe in that. But she believed in birthdays, she said, and she wished Claire bòn fèt.

Claire wanted Madame Gaëlle to keep talking about her mother. But Madame Gaëlle stopped talking. Instead Madame Gaëlle smiled, showing some perfect-looking and long white teeth. Then, as though this were a revelation even to herself, Madame Gaëlle said, 'Your mother *was* my friend.'

Since people said that she and her mother looked so much alike, maybe that's why Madame Gaëlle wanted to be her friend too. And why her father wanted her and Madame Gaëlle to be friends and for Madame Gaëlle to take her.

Tell me more, she wanted to say. Please tell me much more. Open that invisible box with the invisible mother and let me see what is inside. But Madame Gaëlle did not say more. Her smile faded and her face dimmed as if something puzzling were coming into her mind, and she frowned as though the thing that had entered her mind were something that she was trying to make sense of, that she was trying to understand. And Claire now imagined that there might be a similar look on her own face, because she too was trying to figure out whether Madame Gaëlle was now upset. Or maybe Madame Gaëlle was thinking about her daughter. Madame Gaëlle smiled again, as if something had been decided in her mind, and Claire suspected that perhaps Madame Gaëlle's smile was meant to keep her from worrying, and maybe her father had been watching them from somewhere, because at that moment he rose out of the shadows and suddenly he was standing over them, and his shadow covered Madame Gaëlle's body.

Her father had been drinking a little, most likely with the other fishermen around the bonfire. He didn't drink often and never drank a lot, but when he drank he was never happy. She knew most adults got happy when they drank kleren. They laughed and danced by themselves and told jokes. But her father became even quieter when he drank. He became sadder too, as sad as when he was standing at her mother's grave.

Her father's feet seemed to be failing him, as if he were tired of standing over her and Madame Gaëlle, and he sat down on the sand between them. Her father and Madame Gaëlle each seemed to be waiting for the other to talk first, so Claire went back to tugging at her sandal straps and picking tiny grains of sand out from beneath her toenails. While her father had his face turned toward the lighthouse and the hills, Madame Gaëlle said, 'Tonight, I take her.'

Could it be as simple as that? One day she was her father's daughter and the next she was Madame Gaëlle's? And could this really mean that her father was going away for good and that she would never see him again? Would he even come back, like her relatives from the hills, to bring her yams and breadfruit at Christmas?

Her father seemed surprised to hear that Madame Gaëlle was looking to take her that very night. Maybe that's how it was when you got something you'd always wanted but thought you would never get. Maybe her father would be just as shocked when he went somewhere else to live, only to find that chèche lavi, the life he had spent so much time looking for, was no life at all without her.

She tried her best to fight back her tears, kept her hands to her sides as long as she could so her father and Madame Gaëlle would not see her wiping those tears, but the tears came anyway.

'Why now?' her father asked. But why not now, if he was planning to give her away anyway?

'Now or never,' Madame Gaëlle said. And Claire wondered what this meant. Was this the last time the three of them would be together?

Claire looked past Madame Gaëlle and her father, over at the crowd of people still gathered around Madame Josephine. Most of them had known Msye Caleb, just as most of them had known her mother.

She wondered whether her mother would have been able to do what her father was doing, if she would have had the courage to give her away like this, to someone else. She knew of both fathers and mothers, fishing families, who had given their children, both girls and boys, away. They had taken their children to distant relatives in the capital to work as restavèks, child maids or houseboys. Others had taken their children to the white people at Sainte Thérèse and the white people had put the children in orphanages. Some of those children were taken to the capital and other places and were never seen or heard from again. They became other people's children in other lands that they'd never even known existed.

At least she would be staying here, and if her father didn't leave, if he gave up on chèche lavi elsewhere and stayed in Ville Rose, she could visit with him now and then. He would have more time for visits too, because if she was living with Madame Gaëlle, he wouldn't have to work as hard. He wouldn't have to worry about her as much.

'Claire Limyè Lanmè Faustin.' Her father was trying to get her attention. But he didn't even need to call out her name. She was already listening for any word, every word from him. But she did not want to look at him. She did not want to see him sad. She did not want to make him sadder. She thought she heard tears in his voice when he asked Madame Gaëlle, 'You will not change her name?'

This is why he had said her full and entire name. He wanted to remind Madame Gaëlle of it. Claire Limyè Lanmè Faustin. This would always be her name.

And what else, Claire wondered, would he ask Madame Gaëlle to change or not to change about her? She might never sleep in the same place as her father again. Would they even visit the cemetery on her birthday?

Her father was now saying something about a letter he'd given to Madame Gaëlle. Maybe the letter would explain more than he had been able to. Maybe it would make her understand everything. But no words could ever do that. She knew that because even if, like Msye Caleb, she could write the most wonderful letters, she could never write a letter that could explain how she was feeling at that moment.

It was then that she raised her hand. She thought she would pretend she was in school pointing her index finger up to the sky to get their attention. That way, she wouldn't have to look at either of them.

They would also realize that she was always going to be a good girl, that she wasn't going to fight them or disobey, that she would always do what they said. But even if she was going to live with Madame Gaëlle, she wanted her things. She wanted her school notebooks and her uniforms, and even if Madame Gaëlle had fancy beds in her house, she wanted at least the quilt that draped her cot, the quilt her father said had belonged to her mother. So she kept her head down and her hand raised and she told them that she wanted her things, 'Bagay yo.'

Rather than speaking, her father looked in the direction of the shack and pointed to it with an index finger, showing that he agreed she should go get her things.

She wanted to walk the long way, through the crowd, for this was surely her last walk to the shack when it was still hers, but she sensed that both her father and Madame Gaëlle were in a hurry, that they wanted to get the entire thing done with, so she walked quickly, and soon she was opening the unlocked door and peeking inside the shack. But it was pitch-black inside, as dark as when she would wake up in the middle of the night needing the latrine and was too scared to get up even to use the chamber pot. But it wasn't her fear of the dark that prevented her from going all the way in. That darkness was already familiar to her. She knew her way through it.

What kept her from going in was feeling like she had been kicked out, like her home was no longer hers. So she looked back to where her father and Madame Gaëlle were sitting and she noticed they were no longer following her with their eyes. Instead they were each looking at different parts of the beach, trying not to look at each other, so she took advantage of that moment when she knew she was on each of their minds, but in different ways, and she pulled the shack door closed and ran.

She ran through the alley that snaked between the shacks, up to the coco de mer palms at the entrance of a path that led to the lighthouse. Her sandals became entangled in some ylang-ylang creepers that bordered the trail where sandstones turned to hill gravel, then mountain rock. She was relieved when, at last, the trail curved and made an incline up toward Anthère Hill.

Most of the houses on Anthère Hill had high concrete walls topped with bottle shards, conch shells, and bougainvillea vines. The bougainvilleas, she knew, grew so easily, so fast, that they crossed individual walls, creating unintended canopies. The canopied and uncanopied trails zigzagged up toward the lighthouse and Mòn Initil.

The higher she climbed, the breezier it got and the brighter the stars became. The moon seemed larger, more silver than white. The air was much cooler and the sound of the waves faded, though it did not fall away completely. The only voices she now heard were coming from the lighthouse and from the paths between the houses. Muffled conversations were punctuated by giggles from people who sounded as though they were tickling one another.

She heard a dog bark. That bark was echoed by another, then another, until a chorus of barks from large-sounding dogs had been started. Dogs barking – especially big, fat-sounding dogs – always meant you were not welcomed. She heard yardmen's voices hushing the dogs, talking to them as though they were people, telling them to calm down. To be sure she wouldn't be seen, she headed toward the dark, empty houses at the edge of the hill, the newer and larger houses that were occupied only a couple of weeks a year.

She stopped to catch her breath, leaning against the last wall before the hill abruptly ended at a cliff. The wall felt cool against her arm and smooth too, as though it were on the inside of a house. From up there, the view was clear as always, and she could now see part of the beach. She couldn't see her shack or the palms behind it but, even with her eyes closed, she would have been able to point in its direction, along with the bungalow where Msye Sylvain lived with his wife and twelve children and grandchildren. When he wasn't out at sea, Msye Sylvain sold pen tete, breast-shaped bread, which he and his brood baked in a clay oven that was even now flaming.

She couldn't see her father or Madame Gaëlle just then, but she knew where Msye Xavier, the boat builder and metal forger, was, because from the hill the sparks coming from Msye Xavier's tools looked like tiny fireworks. She saw Madame Wilda, who weaved her nets in a low chair behind her house by candlelight. She also saw Msye Caleb's place, because the girl who stayed with Madame Josephine was cooking something, and the girl was illuminated by the cooking fire and the lamp hanging from a post in the outdoor kitchen. Claire saw the white-clad, ghostlike silhouettes of Madame Josephine and her friends from church. These familiar people and the fires that made them visible to her, these points of light, now seemed like beacons calling her home.

But no, she was not thinking of going back.

Suddenly there were more lights. More people were coming forward with lamps. Then one person (her father? was that his voice?) called out her name. Then many others called her name too.

There were so many people calling her name that their voices made their way all the way up the hill to her.

She could hear the men on the gallery of the lighthouse calling out her name too.

She almost answered.

Could this be a song? she wondered. Could her name being called out by dozens of people be a song?

Could it be a new song for her next game of wonn?

For a circle of one.

> Yo t ap chèche li . . .
> They were looking for her
> Like a pebble in a bowl of rice
> They were looking for her
> But no, no, no, she didn't want to be found.

She continued uphill until she found herself on a flat plot of land behind one of the empty Anthère Hill mansions. The land seemed as though it had just been cleared by fire. The earth was still warm beneath her sandals.

Her father liked to say that in a few years Mòn Initil would no longer be useless or initil since very rich people had figured out that they could burn it down, flatten it, and build their big palaces there. Soon it would have to be called Mòn Palè, or Palace Mountain.

She could no longer see the beach, so they wouldn't be able to see her either. She stood for a long time, alone, in the middle of that newly scorched field. Her name was being called from the lighthouse by two or three men whose voices she could easily identify if she thought long enough about it, but she was no longer even tempted to answer.

Maybe they'd think that, like Msye Caleb, she was lost at sea. Her father would be the most worried about her being lost at sea, although he would hide it. He wouldn't show his worry to his friends and neighbors. And not to Madame Gaëlle. But he would no longer have to worry. She would go away. She would go away on her own. She would go where he would never think to come and find her. Like the fugitives in Madame Louise's stories – les marons – she would hide inside what was left of Mòn Initil.

She would be the girl at the foot of the sky. She would find a cave large enough inside Mòn Initil to live in, and at night she would lie on beds of ferns and listen to the bats squeal and the owls moan. She would dig a hole to catch rainwater for drinking and bathing. And she would try very hard not to disturb the marooned spirits who had found refuge there before her. She hoped that there would be no snakes because she was afraid of snakes, though she could learn to live with them if she had to.

But she wouldn't spend all her time there; she would come out every day to watch the beach. She would watch the fishermen go out at daybreak to lay their nets, then return at midday or late in the afternoon. When her father would look up at Mòn Initil from the sea, he would be looking at her without realizing it. He would be sad, but maybe he wouldn't leave the beach or Ville Rose. Maybe he would stay, just as he had when she was living with her mother's family. He might stay close by, waiting, hoping for her to return one day.

She'd heard some of the fishermen's wives say that the spirits of those who'd been lost at sea would sometimes come ashore to whisper in their loved ones' ears. She would make sure he felt her presence too. She'd sneak down at dusk to collect fallen coconuts and grab salted fish left out to dry and she'd stop by and say a few words in her father's ear while he slept. That way she would always be in his dreams. She would go away without really leaving, without losing everything, without dying.

She stood in the middle of the scorched field for a long time, imagining this life as a maroon. She waited for the voices from the lighthouse to die down, until she heard none at all, then she walked past the wildflower field around the lighthouse, and back down through Anthère Hill, to the edge of a much lower butte so that she could see the beach once again.

She was hoping to see her father, hoping to catch one more glimpse of him before she went back up the hill to make her total retreat into Mòn Initil. Then wouldn't he be sorry.

From the lower butte now, she could see that most of the lamps had disappeared, as had the people carrying them. The bonfire had been put out. There were no more lights to be seen, except the moon and the stars and Msye Sylvain's clay oven and Msye Xavier's forging tools and Madame Wilda's candles and net and Madame Josephine's outdoor kitchen lamp. Everyone else, it seemed, had gone in for the night. Or into their own darkness.

Maybe they wouldn't miss her after all.

A warm burst of air brushed past her, rising, it seemed, at that very moment, from the sea. It reminded her of a sensation she sometimes had, of feeling another presence around her: of noticing only one branch of a tree stir while the rest remained still, of hearing the thump of invisible feet landing on the ground, of seeing an extra shadow circling while she was playing wonn. She would sometimes feel the gentle strokes of fingers traveling up and down her back, then lingering ever so lightly at the nape of her neck. She couldn't always pin down the moment these things would start, then stop, so she would call them rèv je klè, waking dreams.

She'd had these types of dreams for as long as she could remember. Soon after they occurred, she would search for signs that something, someone might have actually been there. She would search the ground for footprints, flower petals, sparkly feathers from angel wings. And usually there would be nothing.

But just then, as she was looking down from the butte, she saw Madame Gaëlle running with a lamp in her hand and her shiny, silver-looking gown glowing in the moonlight. And when she saw her father, brightened on the edge of the water by Madame Gaëlle's lamp and satin gown glow, and when she saw other people approaching them with their lamps, forming a circle as if they were a sun, something felt different.

In the middle of the lamp circle, half of which was now in the water, she saw someone pull a man in a red shirt out of the sea. Like a dying fish, the man's body jerked about. Madame Gaëlle and her father were standing together in front of him.

The man reached up, grabbing both her father's and Madame Gaëlle's legs, nearly pulling them both down on top of him. Her father pulled himself back, regaining his balance. Madame Gaëlle fell forward on her knees, landing on the sand near the man. Who was he? she wondered. Could it be Msye Caleb, whom the sea had taken this morning? No. He was gone, they had mourned him, and this man was too wide to be her father's friend.

She thought she heard people shouting her schoolmaster's name: 'Ardin! Ardin!' as if to wake this man from the sea.

She started running farther down the hill, past the jacaranda trees, down to the gravel path, then back through the ylang-ylang vines. Then she stopped on a hibiscus-covered precipice to look down once again. She saw her father and a few other men bend down and join Madame Gaëlle on the sand. They grabbed the man's waist and turned him on his back. Then she saw Madame Gaëlle lower her face and put her mouth on the man's mouth, as though to kiss him.

Her father turned back to face the shacks on the beach.

He was moving his arms wildly, as if to call for more lamps, more people, more help. Or maybe he was simply feeling helpless, feeling just like she was now, afraid.

More people started coming and more lamps. So many people now that they were blocking her view and she could no longer see the red-shirted man, Madame Gaëlle, or her father. She continued down the hill, running so fast that she slipped on some loose gravel stones and fell. She popped back up, then started running again, leaving her sandals behind.

She ran and ran, down toward the alley of coconut palms behind her home.

Fòk li retounen . . .
She had to go back

She thought this too could make a good song for the wonn.

She had to go home
To see the man
Who'd crawled half dead
Out of the sea

She had to go back and see her father and Madame Gaëlle, whose own sorrows could have nearly drowned them. She had to go down to the water to see them take turns breathing into this man, breathing him back to life. Before becoming Madame Gaëlle's daughter, she had to go home, just one last time.

Acknowledgments

I am grateful to the John D. and Catherine T. MacArthur Foundation for the fellowship that gave me the time to attempt this book and so much more. Thanks to my family in Léogâne, those gone and those still there, for introducing me and reintroducing me to the sea.

Mèsi, Fedo, for things that it would take a lifetime to list.

I owe so much to Nicole Aragi and Robin Desser for their love and guidance over nearly two decades now. Thank you, Jennifer Kurdyla, for your time and patience.

The excerpt from the poem 'Le Soleil et les Grenouilles' is from *Les Fables de la Fontaine* (Livre 6), available in various editions. The English translation is mine.

Interview with Edwidge Danticat

by Liesl Schwabe,
June 2013, *Publishers Weekly*

The language in this book is so beautiful and the shifts from English to Creole are so fluid. You grew up speaking French in school and Creole at home, and then, after your family moved to New York, English. When imagining the lives and feelings of your characters, what language do you think in?

I think mostly in English and in Creole. There's a constant flow of translation going on in my head. I hear the characters in whatever language they're speaking – mostly Creole and sometimes also French – and I'm like the scribe in the corner taking notes. You are trained to do this in a family like mine, in which the language you speak depends on whom you're talking to. My daughters are four and eight years old and they sometimes take on these different accents; without realizing they're doing it, they echo the voices of the adults. I feel like when I'm writing, I'm doing a version of that. *Much of this book – both Claire's own story and the story of the town in which she lives – unfolds in reverse, moving from Claire's seventh birthday to her sixth to her fifth, for example. How much do you know about the structure of the book before you start writing and how much of it takes shape as you go?*

I am sometimes an overplanner, but I love it when a book surprises me. This book really surprised me. Everything happens in one evening, and we keep circling back to that evening. Initially I wanted to write a book that was like a radio show, in which each chapter was an episode of that show. But it grew into a lot more – into the story of this little town and some very special people in it.

How often do you return to Haiti these days? How do these visits impact the Haiti portrayed in your fiction?

I still have a lot of family in Haiti so I return quite a bit. I don't go seeking stories, but, like everything you love very deeply, the stories find you.

Your first book, Breath, Eyes, Memory, *was published almost twenty years ago and you've been so prolific ever since. How has your understanding of your own writing evolved?*

I hope that my writing has gotten a lot more nuanced. Things seemed more black and white to me when I was younger. Now I feel I can take smaller stories and really explore them from within. At least I want to keep trying to do that.

Edwidge Danticat

Edwidge Danticat was born and raised in Port-au-Prince, Haiti, and moved to New York when she was twelve years old.

The recipient of a MacArthur 'Genius' Fellowship, she has taught creative writing, worked in film and written for the *New York Times* and the *New Yorker*, in addition to publishing several award-winning books and editing collections of essays and stories.

Equally celebrated for her work in immigrant rights and charity representation, she has received many prestigious honours including the Langston Hughes Award, been a visiting professor at two universities and has spoken at the TED forum.

She lives in Miami, near Little Haiti, with her husband and their two daughters.